YOU ONLY DIE ONCE

YOU ONLY DIE ONCE

Basil Copper

CHIVERS
THORNDIKE

This Large Print book is published by BBC Audiobooks Ltd, Bath, England and by Thorndike Press®, Waterville, Maine, USA.

Published in 2006 in the U.K. by arrangement with the author.

Published in 2006 in the U.S. by arrangement with Basil Copper.

U.K. Hardcover ISBN 1–4056–3659–9 (Chivers Large Print)
U.K. Softcover ISBN 1–4056–3660–2 (Camden Large Print)
U.S. Softcover ISBN 0–7862–8493–5 (British Favorites)

The text of this Large Print edition is unabridged.
Other aspects of the book may vary from the original edition.

Set in 16 pt. New Times Roman.

Printed in Great Britain on acid-free paper.

British Library Cataloguing in Publication Data available

Library of Congress Cataloging-in-Publication Data

Copper, Basil.
　　You only die once : .38 special / by Basil Copper.
　　　　p.　　cm.
　　"Thorndike Press large print British Favorites."
　　ISBN 0–7862–8493–5 (lg. print : sc : alk. paper)
　　1. Private investigators—Fiction. 2. Large type books. I. Title.
　　PR6053.O658Y68 2006
　　823'.914—dc22　　　　　　　　　　　　　　2005037600

CHAPTER ONE

I

'Who the hell's Harry Kettle?' I said.

'He's a small-time film actor who scored a big hit in the lead of Pardon My Truss some years ago,' Stella said.

I gave her one of my enigmatic looks.

'Sophisticated stuff,' I said.

Stella looked at me from under half-closed eyelids.

'You're so Victorian, Mike,' she said. 'The world has moved on since Ronald Colman's day.'

'More's the pity,' I said.

It was one of those mornings in L.A. when even the smog seems to have a sparkle to it and the sun has a golden glow, with an underlying breeze, that tempers the sapping heat it will exhibit later. I looked over toward the window and the stalled traffic on the boulevard. Even the dust outside the pane couldn't diminish the Technicolor qualities of the scene. You're getting another one of your Emily Dickinson moods, Mike, I told myself.

I sat back at my battered broadtop and stared at the cracks in the ceiling. Stella eased her typewriter over and sat buffing her nails in silence with that exemplary tact of hers.

1

Harry Kettle had apparently rung the office before I came and asked to consult me on something. He'd seemed agitated, Stella had said. I wondered what a reasonably successful Hollywood actor would want with a run-down private eye operation like mine. I wouldn't have long to wait; he was due within the hour, so there was no sense in beating my brains out over it.

Despite what I'd told Stella I had vaguely heard of him. He was an early middle-age stand-up comic who'd made a mildly successful TV series a couple of years back and I'd caught one or two of his evening shows. They save peak-time for the blockbusters and big-time movies; the also-rans get the tea-time and the late night slots. That way they're only exposed to children, teenagers and a few night watchmen. It's called programming.

Stella got up with a shirring of nylons that set my animal instincts alight; they're never damped down so far as Stella is concerned though I'd never tell her that. She went over toward the glassed-in alcove where we do the brewing-up, her hair a gold bell beneath the light of the overhead lamp.

'You did want coffee?' she said.

I grinned.

'I didn't say.'

'That's what I thought,' Stella said.

I couldn't work that one out. It was too subtle for me this time of the morning. I sifted through a few letters on my blotter that she'd left for me to sign, salivating like one of Pavlov's dogs. No-one makes coffee the way Stella does and this was always the best moment of the day.

The rest of the time I'd probably be on stake-out or gum-shoe work; when I wasn't getting beaten hell out of and dumped in trash-cans, that is. I pasted what passed for my thoughts together and sat on, brooding over Kettle. There was no doubt he'd sounded a frightened man, Stella had told me.

It was soothing in the office now; the plastic-bladed fan pecked on, redistributing the tired air and even the roar of the stalled traffic on the boulevard was reduced to a quiet mumble.

I set fire to a cigarette, putting the spent match-stalk in the earthenware tray on the desk and watched the languid smoke-rings ascending to the ceiling until Stella came back and put the coffee down on my blotter. Today she was wearing a pale blue two-piece outfit with a pleated jacket, that looked fresh and cool against the tan of her skin. She smiled quietly to herself like she knew what I was thinking and went back to the alcove for the sugar and the tin of our favourite biscuits.

Then she went around the other side of my desk, settled in the client's chair and stared at me unnervingly with very blue eyes. It's a favourite opening gambit with her and I'm always the first to look away. Today was no exception.

'What else do you know about Harry Kettle?' I said.

Stella shrugged.

'If I'd have known he was going to call I'd have brought in my copy of the Movie Buff's Guide,' she said.

Her eyes continued to look at me disconcertingly. I leaned forward to create a diversion and took my first sip of the coffee. Like always it was great.

'Let's make do without,' I said.

Stella put her cup down in the saucer with a faint chinking in the silence. She wrinkled up her nose. On anyone else it would have been disfiguring. On her it looked good.

'You mean his credits, Mike?'

'Anything,' I said. 'His personal habits, for example.'

Stella looked at her small gold wristlet watch.

'He'll be here soon,' she said. 'You'll be able to ask him yourself.'

I grinned.

'I want the sort of stuff he wouldn't tell me.'

Stella shifted easily in her chair, her eyes fastened on my face.

'What makes you think I'd have that sort of information?'

I blew out a small plume of blue smoke at the ceiling, fumigating a bluebottle that was

4

perfecting an Immelman turn about six feet above my desk. He gave an angry buzz and planed down to the far corner of the room.

'You're the brains of this outfit,' I said. 'That makes me think you would.'

Stella gave one of her secret smiles. I could have watched it all day.

'He's on his second divorce,' she said. 'He used to be married to Ashley Ferris. When she was one of the bigger stars.'

'She's still a pretty good comedienne,' I said.

'On TV,' Stella said. 'But the bigger studios won't touch her.'

I stared down at the stalled cars on the boulevard, reaching for the biscuit tin.

'I don't know why we're going into all this,' I said.

Stella had a triumphant look in her eyes now.

'You were the one who wanted to know, remember.'

I didn't answer that. I rooted around in the tin instead, hauling up a couple of my favourite butter-nut fudge specials.

'Anything else?'

I bit cautiously into the outer layer.

'He's been short of money. There was a case in the Examiner a while back. A real estate company was suing him for non-payment of instalments due on a property up on Sunset Canyon.'

'For a girl who's a non-movie specialist you

seem to be doing all right,' I said.

I took another sip of the coffee, looking at Stella as she sat gently smiling in the chair.

'Anything else?' I repeated.

Stella's smile widened.

'Why don't you ask him yourself? He's standing in the waiting-room doorway.'

2

There was a low, embarrassed cough and a darker shadow moved in the waiting-room beyond the office door, which was standing ajar. We hadn't got the light on in there which was why I hadn't noticed him.

'You been talking about me?'

The voice was resentful and suspicious.

'It was nothing libellous,' I said. 'You should be glad of the publicity. My secretary was just telling me how good Pardon My Truss was.'

The door opened wide and a head topped with carroty hair was thrust aggressively into the office.

'This is Faraday Investigations?'

'That's why we had it painted on the door,' I told him.

The little man gave a humourless snigger and came forward into the light. Stella got up and waved him to the client's chair. She went over to her own desk, came back with a light chair and her scratch-pad. She sat down near me and watched the little man.

'I'm Harry Kettle,' he said fiercely, looking from me to Stella.

He sounded so aggressive it was almost funny.

'You got a low boiling point,' I said. 'You want to sit down or stand?'

Kettle had a resigned expression on his face now.

'It's been said before, Mr Faraday. Just skip the jokes about my name. We'll get along a lot better.'

I grinned.

'I didn't know we had any sort of relationship going,' I said.

His grating manner was beginning to get me riled up. Stella shot me a warning glance and rose. She went over to the alcove with quick, rhythmic strides. Kettle went and sat down in the client's chair without saying anything. Stella came back and put the cup of coffee down in front of him. He gave her a grateful glance.

'You must forgive me, Mr Faraday,' he said. 'I been through a rough time lately.'

He put some sugar in his cup and stirred it vigorously. Stella resumed her seat and sat with her scratch-pad in her hand, her gold pencil in the other. Her eyes never left his face. They were misty blue at the moment. I guessed it must be the effect of the overhead lamp combined with the sunlight.

7

'Haven't we all,' I said.

I studied him as he drank. I'd got him now. Though it would have been hard to recognise him as a character who'd once been described as a comic genius to rank with some of the clowns of silent screen comedy. For example, he was much older than I figured. They must have pretty good makeup people at the TV studios.

He must have been pushing sixty though on-screen he looked around thirty-five. I remembered then he was appearing in bit parts in some major Hollywood features in the early forties. So he had to be at least sixty now. He certainly wasn't wearing well and I put the bottle down as being the reason; that and some inner tension that was eating at him.

He had a long, lugubrious face that looked slightly freckled on film but was really heavily wrinkled; he had a face that photographed well though and the lantern jaw and the famous curving lips could be unexpectedly droll when he was fighting back against what the TV writers called 'malign fate.' They're great ones for coining new phrases.

The reddish hair had been carefully tinted to make him look younger and he seemed uneasily conscious about this because he kept putting his hand up to it like he was afraid I knew it. For some reason then I thought of that English actor's great performance in Death in Venice.

Except that the tinting wasn't running down his face there was a good deal of similarity. Give him time, I thought maliciously. It's a warm day. I allowed him a few minutes more to settle himself before starting in.

'My secretary tells me you're in some sort of trouble.'

His lips were twitching now. He looked quite ugly when one came right down to it. Good make-up, lighting and an even better cameraman might turn such features to humour in the right conditions. But he would have to work at it. He certainly wasn't trying for me. He shrugged again. It seemed to be a trademark with him.

'It depends which way you look at it. I been having some problems with my partner.'

'Suppose you start at the beginning,' I said. 'I thought you were a solo turn in movies.'

His eyes expressed surprise.

'There's no money in that any more, Mr Faraday. I've moved into production now.'

'That's a pity,' I said. 'I thought you were great in The Wind in the Banana Trees.'

I saw Stella suddenly overcome by an outburst of coughing. She knew there was no such movie, of course. Kettle looked at me suspiciously but I kept my face straight.

'It's kind of you to say so,' he said unconvincingly. 'This matter concerns my business partner, Herman Stoltz.'

He looked back toward the office door,

9

which was still ajar, like he was afraid he might be lurking there.

'You ever heard of Cesarwich Enterprises, Mr Faraday?'

I sat back at my broadtop, focusing on the cracks in the ceiling.

'It's a conglomerate, isn't it? TV movies, package deals and real estate.'

He nodded, his eyes suddenly shrewd.

'You got it, Mr Faraday. I had some luck a while back. I fell out of movies and into money.'

'That's always nice,' I said.

'There's a lot more to it than that, Mr Faraday. I worked hellishly hard, if I do say so myself. There were three of us originally. One man died and I borrowed money to buy my remaining partner out.'

I transferred my gaze from the ceiling to watch Stella's pen racing across the paper.

'So what's the problem?'

Kettle gave me one of his cautious looks.

'So this, Mr Faraday. At one stage I needed a lot of extra cash to expand or go under. The banks wouldn't help. There's a recession on in Hollywood.'

'I had noticed,' I said, looking down at my scuffed toe-caps.

'That was when I took in Herman Stoltz. He had the cash and the contacts. He was a sleeping partner, really. I did the work and he put up the greenbacks.'

'Are you trying to tell me he's been milking the company?' I said. 'Because if so, you need an accountant . . .'

He interrupted me almost fiercely and there was fear in his eyes now.

'I'm in danger of my life, Mr Faraday. Make no mistake about it, Herman Stoltz is out to murder me.'

CHAPTER TWO

1

There was a long silence in the office, over which I could hear the whine of the bluebottle as it went into a power-dive somewhere up near the ceiling.

'That's a bit strong, isn't it?' I said.

Kettle shook his head. He licked his lips, looking from me to Stella and then back again.

'It's the truth, Mr Faraday.'

I shifted in my swivel chair, staring at the grounds in the bottom of my coffee cup. For once Stella didn't take the hint.

'You want to tell me the story?' I said. 'There's got to be more.'

Kettle swallowed his coffee. There was a gulp in his voice as he replied.

'There's a lot more.'

I spread my hands wide on the blotter.

'That's why we're here, isn't it. For starters, just who is Stoltz?'

There was grudging admiration in Kettle's eyes now.

'He's a smart operator,' he said softly.

'But then so are you,' I told him. 'That makes a matched set.'

Harry Kettle jerked his face into a semblance of a smile. He didn't make a very good job of it. He must have figured that himself because he buried his muzzle in his coffee cup. Stella got the point then. She gave me a smile that lit up the office and went back over to the alcove. I waited until she had settled herself again.

'Who is Herman Stoltz?' I repeated.

'He's about thirty-five,' Kettle said. 'He's a medium to large size operator. He's been in supermarket chains, real estate, that sort of thing. Anything that turns a fast buck. Everything legit and above board, of course.'

'Of course,' I said. 'Otherwise you wouldn't be associated with him.'

Stella buried her face in her notebook again and Kettle started getting white around the eyes.

'Look, Mr Faraday . . .' he began.

'Save it,' I told him. 'Just give me the facts without embroidery. We'll get to the meat a lot quicker that way.'

Kettle gave Stella a despairing glance like he figured she might give him some support but she was scribbling something on her scratch-pad again.

'He's been my partner for about five years. In Cesarwich Enterprises, of course. He comes up with the money O.K. But I figure he's out to take over just when things are beginning to break right.'

'What makes you think that?' I said.

Kettle gave a long sigh. He was pretty good at the enigmatic stuff.

'It looks I got to spell it out for him,' he told the filing cabinet.

I put my fingers round the rim of my coffee cup and studied my nails. That way I stopped my knuckles dancing a tattoo on his skull.

'It's the only way I'm going to find out what you want me to do,' I said.

'A couple weeks ago I had a brake failure on my limousine,' he said. 'I was on the way back from San Berdoo. I don't know if you know the lay-out up there . . .'

'It's hilly country,' I said.

Kettle scowled. He looked as though he could make a good job if he kept at it.

'I was coming down the mountain when it happened. I had to fight the thing for two miles. I just missed a fruit truck on the wrong side of the road before I ran into a lay-by.'

He gulped like he was still tooling the wheel as the landscape came up through the windscreen.

'There was a big pile of sand there, being

used for road repairs. Jeeze! It was a miracle. That was the only thing that could have stopped her.'

'How did you know the brakes didn't fade naturally?' I said.

Kettle spread his hands wide, looking from me to Stella and then back again.

'I got my garage to check her over. Someone had put acid on the cables. It was slow-working stuff and they could have gone at any time.'

I looked at Stella's concentrated blue eyes. She sat with her pencil poised over her notebook, her expression neutral.

'Anyone could have done that,' I said. 'How do you know it was your partner?'

Kettle looked at the cracks in the ceiling. A little bead of sweat trickled down his forehead.

'I feel it in the seat of my pants, Mr Faraday. Intuition, if you like. I just know it's Stoltz.'

'You're going to need a good deal more than that,' I said. 'This agency works on facts. Solid evidence that would stand up under cross-examination.'

Kettle shifted in his chair, gave me a pained look.

'I haven't finished yet, Mr Faraday.'

'You're splitting your infinitives,' I told him. 'But I get what you mean.'

'Stoltz is cunning,' Kettle said. 'So I got to have a good man. That's why I came to you.'

'Now you're talking sense,' I said.

Stella's smile seemed to last a long time before fading.

'He got himself a nice little girl,' Kettle went on moodily. 'She's a high stepper all right. I figure she's one of the reasons.'

'Expensive, is she?' I said.

Kettle smiled briefly. For a while his face was transformed and I had a split-second glimpse of the man who made millions laugh with his carefully timed comedy routines. Leastways, they would once have done so. The kids probably thought it all pretty passé these days.

'You could say that, Mr Faraday.'

'All right, Mr Kettle,' I said. 'You think she's one of the reasons. The girl? She's spending the money so Stoltz wants to take your slice.'

Kettle nodded.

'Now you got it. It's not all the story but it goes a long way. There's been a big change in Stoltz since he met this number around a year ago.'

'I'm still waiting to hear what happened next,' I said.

Kettle gave me another sad look beneath

the tinted red hair, then turned his eyes to Stella.

'I'm waiting to tell you,' he said. 'But you keep asking questions.'

'It's my job,' I told him. 'Just keep the stuff coming.'

Kettle looked helplessly up toward the ceiling. It was a standard ploy and I'd seen him do it a number of times in TV shows. I didn't react to it and he gave it up after a moment or two. I could feel his resentment smouldering in the air and it increased my inner satisfaction.

'Where was I?' he said in the end.

'Acid on the car brake cables,' I said. 'Why didn't you tell the police?'

Kettle's eyes were suddenly alert.

'Have some sense, Mr Faraday. And put my partner wise. Besides . . .'

'You don't like the police, Mr Kettle,' I finished for him.

There were two little red spots burning on the man's cheeks now. They almost exactly matched his hair. For a short moment or two he resembled one of the pierrot figures they sometimes have in those puppet shows that still survive here and there; sometimes in amusement arcades; but more often nowadays in arts festivals mounted on college campuses and at local folk fests.

'You seem bent on misunderstanding me, Mr Faraday. What I meant was that I didn't want the official police in. That would only

16

have brought things to a head and warned Stoltz that I was wise to him.'

'All right, Mr Kettle,' I said. 'Let's start again.'

The little man blew his cheeks in and out once or twice like his temper was getting the better of him. He drummed with his fingers on the blotter. Then he looked at Stella, slowly relaxing.

'Tell you what, Mr Faraday. Go see the people at my garage for starters. They'll tell you about the brake cables. Then come to my office. I'll tell you the rest of the story then.'

His eyes looked at me filmily.

'That way you don't commit yourself. You can take the case or not.'

I glanced at my watch.

'I'll look over there after lunch,' I said. 'Then I'll come on to your office. If you're going to be around.'

He nodded, like he'd lost interest in everything.

'I'm there every day, Mr Faraday. I can understand this must all seem crazy to you. So I got to work on convincing you that it's for real.'

I didn't answer that. He hadn't told me anything really and we'd be there all day the way he was spinning it out. I sat back staring at the ceiling until he'd finished giving Stella the details. She kept her head bent down toward her notepad so I couldn't see the expression

17

on her face.

Kettle finished at last and got up from his chair. He looked at me dubiously.

'It's been an experience, Mr Faraday. I'll expect you later then.'

'Likewise,' I said. 'I'll be there.'

Stella's disapproval seemed to permeate into every corner of the office as she showed the little man out through the waiting room. She came back and looked at me with a neutral expression.

'So we got too many fees coming in this quarter,' she told the filing cabinet.

I grinned.

'He got me riled up,' I said. 'It was his manner or just something about him. Comedians are too sour in private life. I'd rather see him on TV.'

Stella smiled then.

'So why should his partner want to kill him?'

'I'd want to kill him myself if he was around too long,' I said.

I stood her expression for another couple of seconds.

'I'll get to it,' I said. 'That's what this business exists for.'

'I'm glad you remembered,' Stella said. 'I thought it was a philanthropic institution the way you were going on.'

I put my gaze back on the ceiling again.

'You look like a man who could do with another cup of coffee,' Stella said.

'Now you're talking,' I told her.

CHAPTER THREE

1

Acme Autos was a fairly big outfit over on the other side of town, off the main stem but not too far away from the major boulevards. I got across there in half an hour or so, the sun hot on the back of my neck, perspiration making a patch on my shirt where my shoulder-blades met the leather squab of my five-year-old powder-blue Buick. I'm always going to trade the heap in but somehow I never get far enough ahead of the game to put a down payment on something more ritzy.

I found a parking slot in the end and gum-shoed my way down a dusty side-street where a lot of grit and cardboard cartons were dancing about in what passes for the sirocco out here. There was some hassle going on on the forecourt, with automobiles queueing in front of two suites of pumps where characters in bright scarlet overalls wearing scarlet matching baseball caps were making with chrome nozzles and juggling with change.

It looked like the flight-deck of the Nimitz during a World War Two newsreel and I expected Bull Halsey himself to come striding

19

down the concourse any minute. But he never showed and I soon got tired of the display and eased myself into the shade cast by the canopy, wandering over to the cool, dark interior of the repair shops.

There was a lot of noise in here and for a while I couldn't see anything much except for the holes the overhead neon tubes suspended from the roof trusses were burning in the gloom. There seemed to be a lot of work going on and I wandered down the aisles between parked automobiles whose hoods were gaping; and whose entrails were spread across the concrete floor.

I stopped beside a scarlet Pontiac whose radio was blaring out some misty blue thirties tune like they don't make any more; a pair of legs in dirty white coveralls were sprawled into the aisle and there was a light coming from a naked bulb in a rubber and metal guard that was attached to the end of the wandering lead. I waited until the mechanic had finished his inspection and eased back out from under.

He was a tall, thin young man with wispy hair; a long, frank face; and smudges of grease on his nose and cheekbones. He didn't seem surprised and I guessed then he'd seen my feet coming across the concrete from a long way off. He jerked his thumb into the far distance.

'Reception's down there, mister.'

I shook my head.

'I haven't come to pick up a heap. Or check

anything in.'

The boy sat up, putting the lamp down carefully. He wiped his hands on some cotton waste he took from his pocket and rested himself against the Pontiac bodywork.

'I'd like the answers to one or two questions,' I said.

The face was a little more wary now.

'You a cop?'

I shook my head.

'Nothing like that.'

The mechanic grinned, revealing big gaps in his front teeth; he reminded me of something out of an Our Gang comedy of the silent days then.

'Go ahead, mister. It won't cost anything to ask.'

I put one of my size nines up on a beer-crate that stood near the front wing of the Pontiac. I guessed it was used as a seat when these characters had their tea-breaks. My eyes were used to the gloom now. Three other men were working on automobiles in the bays farther down. They didn't even glance at us.

'It's more by way of confirmation,' I said. 'I understand you did a little job recently on a car belonging to Harry Kettle.'

The wispy-haired youth looked at me blankly.

'You know,' I said. 'The comedian. I understand he uses this garage.'

The mechanic scratched his head.

'I remember Mr Kettle. A comedian, you say.'

He grinned suddenly.

'You could have fooled me. I never met a less humorous character.'

'I'm inclined to agree,' I said. 'But that's what they tell me. He had a series on TV.'

The boy looked at me frankly.

'That I got to catch,' he said. 'This information worth anything?'

'I wondered when you'd get to it,' I said.

The boy gave me another view of the gaps in his teeth.

'We all got to live. You didn't tell me your name.'

'I didn't give it,' I said. 'But I'm a friend of Kettle's. He said there was something wrong with his brakes.'

The boy put his cupped hand up to his ear this time. Now he looked like one of the East Side Kids.

'I'm a little hard of hearing today,' he said. 'Must be the racket in here.'

It was my turn to grin. I gave him the ten-spot. He took it so quickly it seemed to melt into the pocket of his overalls. He was serious now.

'I worked on that one, mister. It looked like something nasty.'

He glanced around the workshop like we might be overheard.

'Someone used acid on the cables. They

were about two-thirds burned through before they snapped.'

'You sure about that?' I said.

The boy nodded.

'Sure as I'm sitting here wasting the boss's time.'

'Kettle say what happened?'

The boy in the dirty white coveralls shrugged.

'He was pretty mad all right. And shaken up too. He looked real white. We're really supposed to report those sort of things to the police.'

His eyes were wide.

'You sure you're not police?'

I shook my head.

'I already told you. What did your boss say?'

The mechanic gave me a grimace like something sour was gnawing at him.

'You mean Perrot. He just looks after the business. As long as the money comes he don't say nothing. When he dies they'll have to screw him into the ground.'

A heavy shadow fell across the lighting. I looked up. A big man had come out of a glassed-in office the other side the next bay. He stood glowering at me for a long moment while the wispy-haired boy's legs scrabbled back in underneath the Pontiac again.

I could understand the mechanic's haste. The big character made Sydney Greenstreet look like The Return of the Thin Man. He had four or five chins that got his mouth looking like it was descending into folds of lace. That was the only delicate thing about him. His silvering hair was cut en brosse so that his squat, massive head resembled a pineapple sitting on top of a heap of dumplings.

It was an unappetising analogy but it was all I could think of for the moment. I hated to think what he must have weighed. I expected any minute that the floor would give way but then I remembered we were standing on cement. He had three or four stomachs to match his chins but I could see he had a lot of hard muscle there. He wore a grey silk shirt with the sleeves rolled up to the elbows, revealing arms that were about as thick as my thighs.

His flesh was heavily furred like an animal's and his mauve-tinted bow tie was lost in the shadow of his jowls. He wore a pair of brown-coloured trousers that looked like they'd been cut from an old Zeppelin and his matching suede shoes were so big they looked like canal barges. I expected to see numbers stencilled on their sides but I was disappointed. But then

I couldn't expect everything this afternoon.

His fingers, pink and as big as German sausages, were decorated with a wide assortment of dangerous-looking rings that made me think more of knuckle-dusters than ornament. He had a dark mustache that looked like a dead ferret hanging underneath his nostrils and his eyes, almost lost in the folds of flesh, were the colour of dirty mud. He carried a heavy wooden clipboard in his right hand in such an aggressive way that it looked like a weapon. He was as nice a looking fellow as I'd seen in the last fortnight.

He opened his slit mouth then, coming a little nearer.

'My name's Perrot. I own this joint.'

'That must be nice for you,' I said.

The narrow eyelids closed even tighter over the unblinking eyes.

'Nice enough, mister. Anybody wants any information around here, they come to me. Right?'

'Not right,' I said.

His manner had me riled up.

'I was just having a private conversation,' I said.

The fat man's eyes flickered from me to the mechanic underneath the car. As I watched the legs disappeared with a quicksilver motion. Not that I blamed him.

The big man came even closer. He was amazingly light on his feet for such a bulky person.

'A private conversation about me,' he said softly.

'You must have a bad conscience,' I said.

The fat man's eyes spelled out a signal. My reflexes were well-oiled this afternoon. I had my eyes where they mattered; on his hands. So I ducked, my head a mile away when the big clip-board slammed into a metal filing cabinet in rear of me and split to fragments.

'You must have a heavy bill for broken fittings,' I said.

I moved back as the big man came forward. His balled fist, like a ham-bone made a whistling noise in the air. Leastways, I could have sworn that it did. I chopped him on the side of the neck while he was still off balance. He grunted with surprise, leaning against the bodywork of the auto, fighting for breath. His whole face was a dull mud colour now.

He looked at me like he couldn't believe what had happened. There was murder in the gross features. I decided things had gone far enough.

I got to the big crowbar as he came at me across the greasy cement floor. He stopped so quickly it seemed like his motor had burned out. I held the bar high, measuring the distance to his face.

'I shouldn't try it,' I said pleasantly.

There was white showing around his nostrils by this time. I walked backward slowly, feeling slightly ridiculous. He came down the repair shop toward me, looking as menacing and truculent as a bull. There was a white Rolls-Royce parked up near the entrance of the shop, gleaming and sparkling in the sunlight that spilled through the workshop entrance.

I had a look at the licence details strapped round the steering post. It belonged to Perrot all right. I remembered then that clipboard would have taken my head off if it had gone where he'd aimed it. Perrot was standing stock-still, his big hands clenched. I backed away.

The crowbar bounced twice on the Rolls' bonnet, making two long grooved dents in the coachwork before splintering the windshield. I got out in the sunlight. Perrot was running up now, all control gone.

'I'll kill you if I ever catch up with you,' he screamed.

'It's been tried,' I said.

I got back in the Buick and gunned off the courtyard, keeping the pumps and parked automobiles between him and my rear licence plate. I was still laughing when I got three blocks away. I sobered down then and started making time across town.

CHAPTER FOUR

1

Kettle's place was more imposing than I figured. It was just off one of the main boulevard locations in a fairly chintzy private court development which had an area of sunbaked grass in the centre of the parking concourse and a jaded-looking bronze fountain that was doing its best to cool the surroundings.

I pulled the Buick up in a vacant slot beneath the shade of some well-groomed palms and got out, my grey lightweight suit clinging stickily to my shoulder blades. I slammed the door and went over toward the entrance steps, my shadow stencilled heavily on the dusty tiling.

Like always my toe-caps were scuffed. I sighed. This was like the beginning of a hundred other cases; I seemed to have been ascending the same set of steps for the last ten years or so on my way to unsatisfactory interviews with clients whose problems I brought to some sort of conclusion, usually unsatisfactory.

You're getting old, Mike, I told myself. I always say that at least once on every case and this time I'd decided to say it at the outset and get it over with. It's something to do with being thirty-three; a beat-up P.I.; and with living in a city like L.A. where the heat and the smog seem to strangle initiative and suffocate ambition in all but the most hardy survivors.

I let go of the stale philosophy and pushed open the heavy glazed doors of the entrance lobby to the Dittmar Building; I sensed I'd been here once before on a case a long time ago but I couldn't dredge it up from my brain-box. I drifted over to the far side of the lobby and studied the board screwed to the wall which gave the names of the tenants, their businesses and the locations.

Cesarwich Enterprises had two divisions, like I figured; the TV and film conglomerate was situated on the fifth floor; the real estate branch on the fourth. I decided to try the film division; apart from the fact that it was Harry Kettle's territory, it sounded more exciting; I might get to meet a glamorous blonde or even Francis X. Bushman on his way out. Come to think of it Francis had probably gone out long before I was born.

I waited around with a couple of middle-aged matrons for a vacant elevator and buttoned my way up to the fifth floor. The teak cage stopped every floor to let people on and off; it seemed a busy location. Maybe Harry Kettle would even come up with some money. I began to take a more sanguine view of his assignment; whatever it might be.

I hadn't heard the full story yet. And by the time he'd finished I'd have a clearer view of Stoltz. I'd decided not to say anything about Perrot and his strong personal charm. It would lead only to complications; like an action that might cost me several thousand dollars. My smile lasted me all the way to Kettle's office and drew an alarmed look from one of the matrons with something that looked like a mess of strawberries and cream on top of her hat.

I guessed Perrot maybe did a lot of suspect jobs for people that he wouldn't want the police to know about; and if Kettle needed to avoid his partner's suspicion of his motives, he'd sure as hell have his heap fixed by an outfit like that.

I filed Perrot in that vague territory in back of my mind that sometimes gave out with interesting hunches; he might well do re-sprays on stolen heaps and other jobs for mobs. Like souped up roadsters and the supply of wheelmen. It could be his people had even fixed Kettle's brakes in the first place; and charged the potential victim for putting their own damage right. The irony might appeal to someone like Perrot; it certainly appealed to me.

I was down the corridor now, in front of the polished teak double doors that led to the suite occupied by Cesarwich Enterprises. The faint clittering of expertly pecked typewriters came out from behind the mass of glazing.

I opened up the door and went on in across a thick-pile carpet that caught me behind the knees. A tall, ice-cold blonde wearing a high-gloss bouffant hair-style stood with one manicured hand on the top of a scarlet photo-copying machine and watched me come.

2

Closer up she was even better. She looked like an upmarket version of Eve Arden, if that were possible. She was dressed in a stone-coloured two-piece suit that was cut on severe classical lines and must have cost a lot of money. The only jewellery she wore was a single string of genuine pearls at her throat and an unusual signet ring with an emerald glinting somewhere in the elaborate gold setting.

'Mr Faraday? Mr Kettle said you would be coming.'

'How did you guess?' I said.

She smiled, showing flawless, even teeth. My estimation of Kettle's taste was going up rapidly.

'Mr Kettle gave me a description. Our clients don't usually look like you.'

'I don't know which way to take that,' I said.

The girl smiled again.

'You'll know when you've been around me a

little.'

I raised my eyebrows.

'I'll look forward to that,' I said gallantly.

The tall girl put a warm hand in mine and shook hands formally. I felt her fingers linger for just a fraction longer than necessary. The case was beginning to look up a little.

'I beg your pardon, Mr Faraday,' she said softly. 'My name's Elizabeth Goddard. I'm a director of the company and usually look after things when Harry's away.'

She hesitated.

'Will you step into my office for a few minutes. Mr Kettle's tied up for a while, though he's anxious to see you. I'd like a private talk myself.'

'Surely,' I said.

She led the way across the big office where some half dozen equally ornamental-looking girls were silently surveying us over the tops of their electric typewriters. I admired the Goddard number's action; she had a fifteen jewelled movement that operated with the utmost precision.

She was about thirty I should have said, though she looked a good deal younger; it's something to do with the improved life women lead these days I'm told. I find that a very interesting age for women.

They're out of the callow stage and far more sophisticated and worldly than even girls in the mid-twenties. You should be working for

Uncle Dick's Column on the Examiner, Mike, I told myself.

The Goddard number flung open a polished door which had: ELIZABETH GODDARD: EXECUTIVE VICE-PRESIDENT in gold lettering on the panel. The place was as impressive as the title promised. The floor seemed to be made of black glass in which the white leather divans, tables and rugs appeared to float; it looked like a Paramount film set of the thirties but it was all right with me.

There was a big black glass desk with a white leather top at one end and the chromed blind made a restful twilight of the interior. The girl waved me into a white leather chair that was even more comfortable than it looked.

'I'm just going to have some tea, Mr Faraday. Will you join me?'

'Fine,' I said.

I thought Elizabeth Goddard would ring for a secretary but she was already doing something at a teak-topped working surface that had slid out the far wall. There was a silver teapot and real china cups there. She must have read my expression in the small mirror set over the top because she said softly, 'There is a moment when technology must give way to gracious living, Mr Faraday. One cannot beat the best tea brewed in a silver pot and served in bone china.'

'If you say so,' I told her. 'I get the point.'

I was grinning now. Because there was certainly contrast in my racket. I was thinking of my encounter with the fat man in the garage. From Mickey Spillane to Jane Austen in less than an hour.

'Is one allowed to share the joke, Mr Faraday?' the Goddard number said gravely.

'Sure,' I said. 'It's just that I'm in a gritty business and the gracious bits are few and far between.'

The girl nodded, waiting for an electric kettle to boil. She left it for a moment and came down the room toward me, staring at me unnervingly with very wide brown eyes.

'Don't be put off by Mr Kettle, Mr Faraday. His somewhat rough exterior conceals a good deal of knowledge and culture.'

I stared at her a moment longer.

'I don't doubt it,' I said. 'But I wasn't thinking of him. Just my calling in particular.'

The Goddard number nodded with satisfaction.

'So we understand, Mr Faraday. Mr Kettle looked you up. He wanted the very best.'

'That's flattering,' I said.

'But perfectly true,' she went on calmly.

A column of steam had started rising from the spout of the kettle. As though warned by some inner sense the girl had pivoted quickly and was at the buffet-top with four swift strides. I sat and listened to the clinking of spoons in saucers, taking in the detail of the room.

There was a very handsome bronze trophy on an onyx base set on a mantel shelf behind the girl's desk. It depicted a stallion raised on its hind legs. I made out the incised gold lettering on the base. It said the thing had been presented to Miss Elizabeth Goddard for her services and expertise in the marketing industry by the local Chamber of Commerce. I looked at the girl thoughtfully.

She was obviously a big wheel on the L.A. commercial scene. She had very nice legs too. They seemed to go on for a long time until they were lost to my sight. The girl had been studying me in the mirror because there was a faint pink tinge on each of her cheekbones as she came back down the room with a silver tray.

I wondered what she was thinking. Whatever it was I knew one thing for sure. She was far too good for Kettle. She put the tray down on her blotter and sank into the leather chair in back of her desk. She looked at me casually as she waited for the tea to brew. Then she seemed to make up her mind.

'Mr Kettle's told you something of his problems, of course?'

'A little,' I said. 'I'm here to get the rest now.'

The girl nodded, a look in back of her eyes that was hard to read.

'I may be able to help you there, Mr

Faraday. Mr Kettle's not always an easy man to deal with. And he has a way of putting things that people sometimes find a little . . .'

She hesitated, fishing for the word.

'Abrasive?' I finished for her.

She smiled briefly, reaching out tanned fingers toward the tea-cups.

'Exactly, Mr Faraday. I couldn't have put it better.'

A pink tongue protruded from the corner of her mouth as she carefully poured the tea, assessing its strength and clearness. I saw that she held a silver strainer in her left hand. The whole outfit with the tray would have cost me a year's salary. I figured it for Georgian. You don't live right, Mike, I told myself.

'I think perhaps this character trait may have hampered Mr Kettle's film career,' the Goddard number went on.

'You may be right,' I said. 'But I figure Mr Kettle reached the right niche his talent entitled him to. He had real style and he made maximum use of it. Not many people can say that.'

The girl paused in her pouring and looked at me penetratingly. The faint flush was back on her cheeks now.

'How kind of you to say so, Mr Faraday. I shall convey your sentiments to Mr Kettle.'

'Please don't,' I said, getting up to take my cup from her. 'He might misinterpret my motives.'

The Goddard number had an attractive little crinkle to her nose. She had a whole bag of tricks, come to think of it and I was enjoying them all.

'As you wish, Mr Faraday. Is the tea to your liking?'

'Fine,' I said. 'But shouldn't we be getting to the meat? I don't want to take up too much of your time.'

The girl shook her head firmly.

'My time is carefully apportioned. We are not wasting it.'

'Well, when you've finished assessing my character, I'd like to hear more about Mr Kettle's partner and those dangerous incidents.'

The girl bit her lip. She reached over the desk, picked up a sheet of yellow typing paper. She slid it toward me.

'I've itemised the details there, Mr Faraday. I felt it might clarify things in your mind.'

'That's very helpful,' I said. 'But I'd still like to hear them from you and Mr Kettle.'

The girl nodded, her blonde hair shining in the lamplight. She reached out for her cup, took a tentative sip, her face expressing pleasure. It was pretty good stuff so far as tea goes now that one came to mention it.

'Of course, Mr Faraday. But I'd like you to take that list and peruse it at your leisure.'

She put the cup down with a high, metallic noise that sounded like the chiming of a bell over the faint hum of the air conditioning.

'There is one thing I would like to emphasise before we go on, Mr Faraday.'

She paused and fixed me with those penetrating eyes.

'Sure,' I said. 'That is?'

'Just this, Mr Faraday.'

She picked up the cup again and held it absently in one hand, the steam passing between her face and the overhead lamp making odd little shadows on her skin.

'If you cannot stop the game that is being played, I'm afraid Mr Kettle will be dead within the week.'

CHAPTER FIVE

1

I reached over and picked up my cup with rather more emphasis than I had intended.

'I hope you've got good grounds for such a statement?'

She nodded.

'Reason enough, Mr Faraday.'

I reached out for the sheet of yellow paper, folded it and slipped it in my pocket.

'Aren't you going to read it?' Elizabeth Goddard said.

I shook my head.

'When I get back to the office. Right now I'd like to hear everything from your own lips.'

The girl gave me an impish smile.

'Despite the fact that you'll hear it all again from Mr Kettle?'

'His lips are not so nice as yours,' I said.

The girl put her cup down; she was overtaken by a sudden fit of coughing.

'I'll pretend I didn't hear that,' she said at length.

'Pretend all you like,' I said. 'It's the truth anyway.'

Elizabeth Goddard leaned back in her chair and picked up her cup again.

'I believe you've been to the garage where Mr Kettle took the car.'

I looked at her blandly. This was the tricky bit.

'I went over there,' I said vaguely. 'I made a few inquiries.'

The brown eyes were concentrated on my face now.

'You saw the owner?'

I shook my head.

'He wasn't around. I talked to one of the forecourt staff. I find it more discreet like that. He confirmed what Mr Kettle said, of course.'

I needn't have bothered. The Goddard number merely nodded. Her mind was obviously miles away. Now all I had to do was to steer Kettle's thoughts off the subject.

'Of course,' the blonde number repeated.

She fixed me with one of her best glances. She was in danger of hypnotising me if she went on like this. I could have stood it all right.

'I must just emphasise one thing at the outset, Mr Faraday. Mr Stoltz is a brilliant man. He did a lot for the business when he first came in by way of cash injections. Later he personally engaged his considerable talent.'

'So Mr Kettle hinted,' I said.

Elizabeth Goddard ran a pink tongue round her lips.

'One must give the devil his due.'

I didn't say anything, just went on sipping the tea and waiting for her to continue. Her eyes flickered across my face like she was checking whether I was paying proper attention. She needn't have worried. Her personality was such that one couldn't fail to get the message.

'And Mr Stoltz is a very personable character. He gives an extremely reasonable, civilised and charming image to the outside world.'

'So the scales are loaded against Mr Kettle,' I said.

The Goddard number's eyes flickered briefly across me again but her voice was soft and mild when she replied.

'I'm just trying to balance things up, Mr Faraday. So that you can get a clearer picture.'

She leaned forward and examined her well-manicured nails against the background of the blotter.

'I'm an outsider and can give an unjaundiced view.'

'You're not really an outsider,' I said. 'You have a vested interest.'

The blonde girl went on examining her nails. The even timbre of her voice didn't change.

'That is true to a certain extent, Mr Faraday. I am a partner, as you so very reasonably point out. So my fortunes are bound up with Cesarwich Enterprises. But I think I am objective enough to see who is at fault in this delicate situation. I am just going to particularise. And I think I know enough to confirm what I said before; that Mr Kettle is in considerable danger.'

'We've heard about the brakes,' I said. 'What next?'

Elizabeth Goddard still seemed extraordinarily interested in her manicure. The edges of the silence in here were frayed now by the faint pecking of the distant typewriters in the outer office.

'You'll find it itemised on your list,' she went on. 'How about a cliff-slide for openers?'

2

The smoke from my cigarette went up blue and unwavering toward the ceiling in the still

41

air, as my pen scratched on across the paper.

'You're sure about this?' I said.

The blonde number nodded.

'I was there. The four of us had gone out to do a survey on this property. Harry was standing about ten yards from me, underneath this bluff. Herman and his girl-friend, Pepper Coburn, had disappeared somewhere temporarily. I looked up to see this mass of rock and stuff coming down. I shouted and Harry jumped out the way just in time. There must have been fifty tons of rubble piled on the place where he was standing. He would have been crushed to pulp.'

'The fall could have been accidental,' I said.

The girl shook her head.

'We had a look at the bluff later. The edge looked like it had been levered away with something like crowbars. Besides, like I said, I caught a glimpse of Stoltz up there just before the fall.'

I shook my head, riffling back through the notes.

'Not entirely correct,' I said. 'You caught a glimpse of someone wearing a check pattern sport jacket. Stoltz was wearing a similar jacket that afternoon.'

The girl shrugged.

'Think what you like, Mr Faraday. I'm sure in my own mind.'

I grinned.

'Take no notice, Miss Goddard. It's my job

to ask questions. And you say the couple appeared from the direction of the house about a quarter of an hour later?'

'That's right,' Elizabeth Goddard said defensively. 'But they could have worked round there from the bluff. The property is up on Durango Drive. The house is empty, you see, so there was no-one to corroborate or deny their story. Harry didn't want to make anything of it so we passed it off as a landslip.'

'We'll set that aside for the moment,' I said. 'I'll read it up later. What next?'

'The elevator,' the girl said. 'One of those in this building. Harry was working late that night. Stoltz had gone home about half an hour earlier. The lights went out as he was walking down the corridor.'

'That's not usual?' I said.

The girl shook her head.

'Never happened before. Harry thought a fuse had gone. It was very dark but there was a faint light from the neons and street lighting filtering in and he got to the elevator. He buttoned it and it seemed to be working all right, because he heard it coming up. At the same time there appeared to be someone mounting the stairs in the darkness.'

I was silent for a moment, watching my cigarette smoke slowly ascending. The girl rose to pour me another cup of tea.

'He tried the lights in the corridor?'

'Surely. They weren't working at all. He

opened the elevator doors and went to step inside. There was nothing there.'

Elizabeth Goddard's face was white now. I could see a small muscle working in her throat.

'Nothing but the empty elevator shaft and a hundred and fifty feet drop to the concrete. The cage itself was on the next floor up because he checked later. If he hadn't grabbed the grille he would have been a dead man. He was so shocked it took him a couple of minutes to claw himself back into the corridor.'

'Nasty,' I said. 'That might take a considerable knowledge of electronics if deliberate.'

The blonde girl nodded.

'Herman Stoltz has a very extensive knowledge of electronics, Mr Faraday, believe you me.'

'And the man coming up the stairs?'

The girl's face was still pale.

'He turned around. Harry was making a considerable noise. Harry heard the footsteps going down very fast as he was fighting to keep his hold on the metal grille. The lights came on soon after.'

'Suspicious,' I said. 'But still circumstantial. He didn't really see anyone.'

The Goddard woman shook her head.

'You're a hard man to convince, Mr Faraday.'

'I'm looking for facts,' I said. 'So far it's all supposition. Why has Harry never tackled his partner head-on about all this?'

The blonde girl looked off balance for a moment.

'I thought he told you his reasons, Mr Faraday. In any case you'll be seeing him in a few minutes. Why don't you ask him?'

'I shall,' I said. 'And he did give me some of his ideas. But it's difficult to understand. For an outsider.'

The girl's eyes were grim now.

'You don't know much about business, Mr Faraday. There are many silent struggles for power going on in outfits like Cesarwich, especially in today's difficult economic climate. People have murdered before now to gain control.'

I leaned back in my chair.

'I'm open to convincing, Miss Goddard.'

The girl's eyes were ironic now.

'I think this would convince even you, Mr Faraday.'

She eased forward at the desk, lowering her voice like we were the conspirators in some old Sydney Greenstreet movie. You're repeating yourself, Mike, I told myself; you've already had Sydney Greenstreet once this afternoon.

'It happened only two days ago and was the clincher so far as Mr Kettle was concerned.'

I put down my cup and picked up my pen again, glancing at the sub-heads I'd scribbled in the notebook. I'd check them out against the typed stuff later. The girl was still drinking her tea like we had all the time in the world.

'He and Mr Stoltz had gone over to some property the company owns on the edge of town. It's a deep-freeze plant which serves a wide area. You know the sort of thing. The buildings cover several acres and refrigerated trucks turn up to collect material for retail distribution.'

'Why were the two men together on this occasion?' I said. 'Especially if Mr Kettle suspected his partner.'

The girl shook her head, slight impatience showing in her eyes.

'Mr Kettle had never let Mr Stoltz become aware of the slightest suspicion on his part,' she said. 'If you knew him better . . .'

'You already said that,' I told her. 'I get your point. So here were these two men, one trying to kill the other. The first keeping up a façade, the second pretending to be unaware of the true situation.'

The Goddard number shot me a penetrating look from the wide brown eyes.

'You've encapsulated it well, Mr Faraday. There was another reason they were there together. Cesarwich has the possibility of greatly enlarging its capacity on the site. They had come to inspect a new type of freezer chamber which had been installed. And they wanted to measure up and estimate the available land for new warehouses and parking

46

bays.'

'So?' I said.

The blonde girl paused, one tanned hand resting delicately on the handle of her cup.

'They had all the legal papers with them. Both their signatures were needed. And Mr Stoltz was flying up to San Francisco the following morning.'

I nodded.

'So what happened?'

The Goddard girl turned down the corners of her mouth. It didn't affect her beauty any.

'After they had finished measuring and had signed the papers, Harry put the stuff away in his briefcase. Then they inspected the new freezer chambers together. They're big places and as they walked round the various bays and aisles the two men became separated. When they went into the second one Stoltz said he'd check the third in order to save time. Harry went on, thinking nothing of it. Presently he finished the inspection and he was getting pretty cold.'

The girl let go the handle of her cup and licked her lips.

'It was then he found the entrance door closed. There's an emergency handle on the inside but that had either jammed or been put out of action.'

I sat staring at her for a long second.

'Nicely done,' I said. 'But surely he could have made himself heard.'

47

The Goddard number shook her head.

'Those doors are very heavy and thick. It's difficult to make oneself heard from inside. And there's an elaborate bar and lock mechanism on the outside linked to an alarm system to deter theft.'

'He obviously survived,' I said. 'So you tell me what happened.'

Elizabeth Goddard gave me a tight-lipped smile.

'I forgot to tell you, Mr Faraday. It was a Sunday and there was no-one working there, apart from the two watchmen who would be relieved by the night security guards. There was no meat stored in that chamber so Harry could have frozen to death. The freezer chamber was working up to its correct temperature. Or down if you prefer.'

I made another note on my pad.

'He could have been there for weeks?'

'Exactly. But a truckie came out there, purely by chance, on an emergency pick-up of frozen meat. He made a mistake and came to the wrong bay. He opened the door and let Harry out. He'd been there for three hours and was in a pretty bad way by then.'

'Mr Stoltz had left the site?' I said.

'He'd been talking in the factory office to one of the watchmen,' the blonde girl said. 'A phone call came through for him with an urgent message. He asked the man to tell Harry he'd been called away but that he'd ring him from Frisco.'

I leaned over and put the stub of my cigarette in the onyx tray on the girl's desk.

'Kettle's car would have been parked outside the complex.'

The girl nodded.

'That's the clever part of it, Mr Faraday. There are over two hundred freezer chambers on that site. And the place where Harry was trapped wasn't even in use. There'd be no real need for the staff to go there. And in the meantime Stoltz had gone up the coast.'

'It seems like a fifty-fifty business to me,' I said. 'The watchman may have spotted the car, known it was Kettle's and checked the whole site out.'

'Or they may have figured he'd gone off in Stoltz' car for some reason,' the girl said softly. 'Mr Kettle's in no doubt he would have died in there if it hadn't been for that truckie coming.'

'You may well be right,' I said. 'But we've still got no proof of anything.'

The girl smiled.

'That's why you're here, Mr Faraday. To provide proof.'

'I'll do my best,' I said.

The girl seemed to recollect something and pushed a sealed envelope across the blotter toward me.

'Mr Kettle left this for you, Mr Faraday. It's a retainer. If you want more you have only to ask.'

I picked up the envelope like it might burn a hole in my fingertips. I hoped Kettle felt in a generous mood today. If he figured he had only a week to live he might be.

'Of course your inquiries will be discreet, Mr Faraday. Mr Stoltz mustn't know he's suspected. So that rules out the direct approach.'

'I knew this assignment was going to be too easy,' I said.

The girl smiled again.

'Mr Kettle will tell you all about the rest. I wish you luck.'

'I'm going to need it,' I said.

I got up. It was then I noticed that a door at the far end of the office and slightly in rear of me was half-open. Harry Kettle was lounging in the opening, watching me and the girl silently. His eyes were like two black holes in the whiteness of his face as I went on down the room toward him.

CHAPTER SIX

1

I studied the cheque for the fifth time. It seemed to have a lot of noughts on it.

'So we get to eat again?' Stella said happily. The gold bell of her hair shimmered underneath the lamps as she leaned over me, watching while I scribbled my name on the reverse. The neons were making a mottled pattern of red, green and gold at the window in the gathering dusk.

She took the slip of paper in her slim fingers and studied it frowningly.

'I'll pay it in first thing in the morning, Mike.'

I sat back at my old broadtop as her heels clittered over toward the alcove. I caught the fresh aroma of the coffee as she fooled with cups and saucers. The tea had been fine in its way but the day was getting back into its stride again now. I went over and locked the waiting room door while she was getting the biscuits. Then I got back to my chair, watching Stella's face through the ascending steam from my cup.

She had the sheet of yellow paper the girl had given me and was studying it concentratedly.

'Not really a lot to link this with Stoltz, Mike,' she said in the end.

'That's what I figured,' I said. 'Like I told the girl and Kettle, it's all pretty circumstantial. Though both of them are convinced it was Stoltz up on the bluff when those rocks came down.'

'He didn't tackle him about the freezer incident?' Stella said.

I shook my head.

51

'He says it would have tipped his hand. And it is just possible one of the watchmen shut that door quite innocently, without realising anyone was in there.'

'If Stoltz is behind all this he's playing his hand cleverly, Mike,' said Stella, tapping with her gold pencil on very white teeth.

I picked up my cup and took another sip of the brew. It was one of her best efforts.

'I'm not quite sure of the financial side,' Stella said. 'Or exactly why Stoltz wants full control.'

'It's complicated,' I said. 'Kettle threw a lot of figures at me but finance isn't my strong suit. What you have in your notes is about the strength of it. A whole range of accidents in any one of which Kettle could have been killed. And an intuition about his partner's financial ambitions.'

'And you have to play it discreetly,' Stella said. 'It doesn't give you much room for manoeuvre.'

I grinned.

'That's why I want your opinion, honey.'

Stella put her head on one side and looked at me with very blue eyes. It was one of the looks that seems to penetrate to the soul and I stood it for only a few seconds. I plunged my face into my coffee cup again while Stella bent to the yellow sheet with a quiet smile of triumph.

'One or two things do suggest themselves.'

'Suggest them,' I said. 'I'm fresh out of ideas myself.'

Stella shot me a look of slight irritation.

'You'll have to come up with something by tomorrow, Mike.'

I swivelled in my chair, looking up at the cracks in the ceiling.

'I'll have a hold on myself by then,' I promised her.

'I found one or two starters for you,' Stella said quietly.

I took my eyes away from the ceiling and focused up on her.

'Like what?'

'I rang up Stoltz' home a while back,' she said.

I stared at her for a long moment.

'You want to blow the whole thing?'

There was a slight flush on Stella's face now and her jaw had set stubbornly.

'You ought to know me better than that, Mike.'

I shifted uncomfortably in the swivel chair. She was right, though.

'Apologies in advance,' I said. 'What's the story?'

Stella smiled briefly.

'I looked up some of Cesarwich' new property deals in the Examiner and other sheets. They're developing estates all over the place. I was Mrs Joyce Cochrane who was interested in a two swim-pool lay-out up in the

Holmby Hills.'

I stared at her with glazed eyes.

'Two swim-pools?'

'That's what I said,' Stella told me quietly. 'You really are out of touch. One can't have a house these days without a servants' bungalow. And no self-respecting servants would take such a position unless they had their own swim-pool.'

'My,' I said. 'I'm really back in the eighteenth century. Maybe I ought to apply for a butler's job myself.'

Stella shook her head, a shaft of neon making a brief green shimmer on her hair.

'You're not the type, Mike. Where was I?'

'Buying a two million dollar property off Herman Stoltz,' I said.

'I told him I was sorry to bother him at home,' Stella went on, 'But I simply had to have the place. To make a short story shorter he said he'd be home all day tomorrow. He lives at a big spread called The Grange. I thought you might look over there.'

'For what purpose?' I said. 'He's expecting you. He won't be thrilled with me.'

Stella gave me one of her long-suffering looks.

'You won't be going inside, goof. I thought you could see who comes and goes. Get an idea of the situation. Kettle doesn't want you to make any direct approaches.'

'Another stake-out,' I said. 'Great.'

Stella's teeth were very white in her smile.

'You have any better ideas?'

I looked at her again, pushing over my cup. She took the hint and went back for re-fill. I waited until she'd re-seated herself.

'I'll go over there tonight,' I said, answering her question.

Stella shook the hair back from her forehead, looking from me to the plastic-bladed fan that was redistributing the tired air and then back to me again.

'Any special reason?'

'A very good one,' I told her. 'A lot more things happen at night than in the day-time and I might as well start in spending Kettle's money right away.'

She didn't argue with that.

2

I had the large-scale of L.A. taped to the dashboard of the Buick and I didn't have much trouble locating the section. I got over to the canyon where Stoltz lived in under the hour. There'd been a photograph of him and Kettle wearing hard hats at the inauguration of some building project hanging in Kettle's office and I thought I would recognise him again.

I didn't really know why I was coming out here but I had to start somewhere and I always play things by ear. And like I'd told Stella a lot more things do happen at night and not only from a sexual angle. From any angle when you get right down to it.

I'd chewed things over with Stella for a while, concentrating mainly on my second interview with Kettle but we hadn't settled on anything. Like the Goddard number had said he was a badly frightened man. I'd figured that out already. But it didn't help me any. His suspicions of his partner were based on whispers given him by friends and business associates.

Some funds had been sliding from account to account but I'm no financial wizard and the stuff he'd put on the desk in front of me didn't mean a thing; they were photo-copies of bank statements; accounts of various businesses in which the two men were concerned; and printed financial estimates on glossy brochures relating to various large-scale ventures in which Cesarwich was involved.

Like Kettle had hinted it was a seat-of-the pants intuition but I felt that if I'd been in his position I'd maybe feel insecure and persecuted too. From what he'd told me he figured that he'd only got another week to go if the rate of the attempts on his life kept up. His luck was bound to run out sooner or later; I granted him that.

But it didn't give me much to go on. Most of what he told me was suspicion based on hints; conversations with Stoltz into which he'd read deeper meaning than I could fathom; and, unfortunately for me, he had no real evidence that Stoltz had been a hundred per cent responsible for all the things that had happened to him.

He thought he had seen a man in a similar sport-jacket on the bluff before the cliff came down; but that could have been sunlight on dappled leaves. And the bluff could have collapsed of its own accord; all the California coastal section is a slide area. He hadn't seen anyone near the elevator; only heard someone ascending and descending the stairs.

Similarly, anyone could have put acid on the brakes; but that was a reality because the boy in the garage repair shop had confirmed it. And it was just possible there could have been some misunderstanding out at the freezer plant; that one of the watchmen had shut the door inadvertently with Kettle inside. Though the phone call to Stoltz in the office while the watchman was there could easily be checked.

But I didn't want to go out to the freezer plant. Not yet at any rate. That would only draw attention to myself in such an isolated location. On reflection I thought Stella's idea might be best for starters. Interesting things had transpired in the past from such mundane beginnings.

I was just turning the Buick up into the hills at this point when the first flicker of lightning split the horizon. I found the intersection and drummed on over the uneven surface of the secondary road, still going uphill, when the rain began.

That figures, Mike, I said. I seemed to have spent most of my life on stake-out with heavy rain sluicing down the storm-drains. It looked like one of those sudden flash-storms we get in Southern California.

They last an hour or so and do a lot of damage sometimes but the strength and volume of the rain seldom keeps up for any real length of time.

I switched on the wipers and went on down, glancing at the map and looking out the side-window for the property I wanted. It looked like it might be difficult to find under these conditions because the windshield was a mass of running water now and it had long been dark. There were few lights in what was little more than a rural lane and I couldn't make out the details of the name-boards even when they were visible.

I pulled the Buick in under some sheltering trees and killed the lights. Fortunately, I had a raincoat on the back seat which I usually keep there and I put it on now, listening to the drumming urgency of the rain on the roof. By the occasional lightning flash I could see solid sheets of water coursing down the gutters.

I sat there for a couple of minutes longer, but there didn't seem to be any slackening. I either had to go on with what I'd set out to do or give up. I'm not one to give up so I stayed put for a couple more minutes, smoked a quick cigarette and thought things over. Then I left my half-smoked butt in the dashboard tray, got out into the gusting rain and pounded over the streaming pavement to the nearest gateway.

It was the entrance to an imposing drive, with a brick-built lodge that looked dark and deserted. The booming rumble of thunder echoed across the distant hills, ending in a splintering crash that sounded like a fireball had struck something somewhere. Then there was an eye-searing flash that made the entire lane visible in its yellow glare.

I was pretty wet by now but the flash lasted just long enough for me to make out the lettering incised in the great stone pillar in front of me. It said: THE GRANGE.

I was back in the driving seat of the Buick in three seconds flat, water running down my collar, my raincoat sticking soddenly to my suit. But I had a lopsided smile on my face as I finished off my cigarette and waited for the rain to die out.

CHAPTER SEVEN

1

I sat there for about an hour but there was no sense in moving until the worst of the storm had passed. My clothing had dried out and I was on my third smoke before the rain eased off. I checked my watch. It was early evening still and I had plenty of time. I left the Buick where it was; it was a little near to the entrance of The Grange but well into the shadow and if anyone did come along its position was ambiguous.

The owner might have been intending to visit any one of half a dozen houses round about; the gardens were big and sometimes covered several acres—almost enough in some cases to be called estates—but I'd noticed several roofs poking above the trees within a few hundred yards and I didn't think my heap would arouse any suspicion.

Not that anyone was likely to come poking around, particularly on foot, on such an evening. The rain had stopped now. I got out the driving seat quietly, closing the door after me with a barely audible click. I gum-shoed over toward The Grange, keeping my eyes peeled for any signs of life in the entrance lodge.

There were none and I guessed that maybe it was disused at the present time; the impression was reinforced by the big iron double gates which were drawn back from the pillars and fixed with metal bolts into sockets in the tarmac. There was no-one around and no sound apart from the distant whine of a jet, probably an air-liner circling to land at L.A. International.

I walked past the lodge quickly, keeping my face buried in my collar, just in case there was anyone around. There was a damp, unhealthy stench on the wind like leafmould or rotting vegetable matter that hadn't been disturbed for a long time. My shoes were making rather too much noise on the hard surface of the drive and I got off on to the grass verge as quickly as possible.

It was colder than I figured up here and the breeze, bearing with it the moisture, seemed to penetrate my thin raincoat right to the bone. There was a little more light in the sky now and I kept on walking briskly, glad of the slight warmth the exercise engendered.

I had no way of knowing whether Stoltz was even home this evening. Stella had spoken to him at his house in the late afternoon, of course, but he may have gone back in to L.A. since then. Apart from a wasted journey and some discomfort it hadn't cost me anything.

I had turned a slight left-hand bend in the drive now and my eyes were adjusted to the light; I could see that the whole stretch of tarmac in front of me was clear. There was a pale moon out, riding beyond the edge of the ragged clouds, and its faint light struck crystal reflections from tree branches and thousands of leaves of the foliage that fringed the drive.

You're getting poetic again, Mike, I told myself; but I had nothing else to divert myself with for the moment and it was one way of passing the time. The drive jinked again and I went on round, hands thrust deep in my pockets, my breath smoking out my mouth it was so cold up here, keeping on the grass verge. There was still nothing but the black surface of the tarmac; the drive winding on in the moonlight; and the impenetrable shrubbery each side.

I went on round the next bend and things started opening up; the drive itself became wider; the trees dropped away and I could see moisture sparkling on the grass of a vast, shaved lawn that went away in shallow curves toward a big, low white house that sat atop a mound in the far distance.

There were lights pricking the façade and a series of expensive-looking bronze lamp-posts fringing the driveway, which curved round the edge of the lawn to the foot of an imposing set of steps that led up to the main entrance. The lights atop the posts weren't lit.

I looked round the whole area in the paleness of the moonlight. Nothing moved in all the expanse except for the faint stir of branches in the night breeze. I got over toward the house as fast as I could, bending low and keeping to the grass. There were two big automobiles parked near the foot of the steps, close to several sets of white-painted doors set into the face of the bank, which obviously led to garages.

I hoped there was no-one sitting in the vehicles. I was relying on the owners being inside the house. I was right on this occasion. The lights of the mansion had disappeared now, cut off by the bulk of the mound that had reared itself to block out a good deal of the sky. I didn't waste any time finding a way around but went up the steps two at a time.

There was a broad, stone-flagged path at the top that led straight to the main entrance of the house; I got off it quick, keeping behind one of the rows of ornamental trees that flanked the path. I went across a smaller lawn diagonally, keeping in the thick shadow cast by the trees. There was a set of four French doors punched into the façade away to my right that were lit, throwing the fretwork patterns of the window bars on to the terrace.

It indicated a pretty big room and one likely to be occupied because of the lights. I was going more slowly, unwilling to commit myself to the brightly lit expanse of lawn until I was certain there was no-one inside looking out. In the end I went back, keeping in the shadows of the ornamental trees at the main path and then worked my way along the façade.

There were lights only in the entrance porch; in the room with the French doors and in one upstairs window. I walked slowly down the terrace, crouching below the window levels of rooms which were in darkness. I was convinced no-one could know I was here but I make my living and keep my health through taking care and tonight was no exception.

I didn't know Stoltz and he didn't know me but if only half of what the girl and Kettle had said was true then he could be my enemy as well. And my presence in his grounds at night, trying to look through his windows, could take some explaining. I was up near the big casements now and I eased forward, taking care to prevent my shadow falling across the terrace.

From what I could see the room was enormous; it was got up as a library, with thousands of leather-bound volumes marching round the shelves and across the two walls that were visible. There was also a massive wooden gallery that ran round the top of the room and that had an openwork balcony and fitted book-shelves too.

I took a couple of steps forward and risked a glance close-up, momentarily taking in most of the room, except for the near-side wall. So far as I could make out it was empty for the moment. I took another glance at my watch and settled down to wait.

2

It wasn't too long before something happened.
It must have been a quarter of an hour or so
and I was getting pretty cramped squatting on
my haunches. But the rain kept off and my
slicker had dried on me.

I wasn't conscious of anything specific at
first, but then I heard a faint tune that was
vibrating at the window panes. A shadow
moved across the white-wood shelving of the
library. I risked a quick glimpse. A tall man in
a white tropical suit was standing by a large
table on which a lot of bottles stood. He was
fooling around mixing drinks and I had time to
study him.

I had no doubt it was Herman Stoltz
because Kettle had described him during our
conversation, and like I said I'd noticed his
picture. Despite this the reality was a little
different to what I had imagined. He was
around thirty-five, well built; lean and athletic.
His tanned face was smooth and unlined and
his blond hair, which was cropped fashionably
short, displayed no trace of grey.

He had a clipped black mustache and very
even white teeth. His scarlet bow-tie made a
vivid splash of colour under his chin as he
moved farther forward across the room,

65

holding out a glass to the girl who came out into the centre of the library toward him.

I guessed then she'd been sitting in an easy chair to one side of the great stone fireplace I could glimpse in the gold-framed mirror that was hanging between two of the big bookcases opposite. I was glad then I hadn't gotten closer to the window or stepped out from the shelter of the brickwork.

The girl's presence had been masked by the fact that she'd been sitting close to the wall which contained the windows and I wouldn't have known she was there until it was too late. It was probably she who had switched on the radio or record player because Stoltz had evidently just come in from the hallway outside.

The girl who came forward to take the proffered glass was presumably Pepper Coburn, the woman Elizabeth Goddard had mentioned. I vaguely remembered her face from some re-runs of fairly prestigious movies I'd seen on TV within the last year or two. I'd get Stella to check from her reference books in the morning.

She was of medium height but because of her slimness and the length of her legs she looked a good deal taller. She was dressed in a lightweight grey tailored suit which clung and moulded itself to her outstanding figure as she came down the room. That brave vibration each way free, as the poet puts it. I think it was

Andrew Marvell but I couldn't be sure this evening, crouched in the darkness of Stoltz's damp garden.

A fine point, Mike, I told myself. And something to take a raincheck on. For the moment I'd take the reality in preference to the printed page. But that glittering certainty taketh me. The girl had her back to me now but then she turned in profile and I was certain it was the Coburn number.

The two toasted one another in silence before coming on down the room to where large leather divans and easy chairs were set about. They had halved the distance now and I was able to take in greater detail. Stoltz sat sidewise on to me in one of the easy chairs, draping one leg casually over the arm.

The girl went to sit on the divan immediately facing me. I got down toward the bottom of the window and hoped there wasn't enough light spilling out across the terrace tiling to make my face visible to the people in the room. I didn't think so because there was a table up near the glass, which cast a lot of shadow, but I wanted to be careful tonight.

At one stage I obviously had to present myself to Stoltz and I didn't want to tip my hand. The wind was rising again now, making a faint fretting noise in the branches of the ornamental tree above my head. I glanced quickly up and down the terrace but everything was dead and deserted just like it had been since I came in here.

I hadn't learned much tonight but at least I would recognise Kettle's partner and his girl-friend next time I saw them. And tonight's operation was merely intended to be a reconnaissance. I shifted my position again, easing a cramp in my knee and withdrawing into a patch of darker shadow.

When I looked again the man and the girl in the library were deep in conversation; disappointingly I couldn't make anything of it. They were too far away and in any event their voices came merely as faint vibrations above the music from the record player. I shifted my balance, taking the weight of my body on my other leg and gave another glance at my watch.

The conversation seemed to be absorbing. Presently Stoltz got up and wandered out of my field of vision. The music stopped abruptly. He'd obviously switched the machine off. He came back again and the conversation resumed. The girl had a small black notebook out by this time and they sat side by side on the divan, studying it as though comparing detail.

I had my ear close to the window glass, oblivious of the film of moisture clinging to it. I still couldn't make out any tangible sentences. It was one of the most frustrating situations I'd ever been in.

I straightened up in the end. Unless something dramatic happened it was pointless me staying here. If the weather had been normal I'd have done better on stakeout. But it didn't seem to me as though many people would come to visit Stoltz out here. If he'd planned his partner's murder he'd have to have accomplices. And in that case they'd be less conspicuous visiting his office. That way they would merge in the crowd.

What was it Kettle had said. That Stoltz looked mainly after the estate and property side of the conglomerate? That might be more profitable in the morning. In the meantime I was hungry, cramped and damp. It was time to move.

I was still crouched there with these and a few other things on my mind when there was a whispering exhalation in the darkness and something tore a sliver of bark off the trunk of the tree a couple of feet above my head.

CHAPTER EIGHT

1

I rolled over wet grass, reaching for a Smith-Wesson that wasn't there. It hadn't been that sort of case—yet. The .38 was in the locked cupboard of the small armoury I keep in the bedroom of my rented house over on Park West. I kept on rolling, the sweat of fear mingling with the moisture from the grass on my face.

I was in darkness now, my eyes searching for something that would locate the character who'd tried to take me out. As I'd rolled away I'd seen Stoltz and his girl-friend still deep in conversation. They obviously hadn't noticed a thing.

The shot had come from farther along the façade of the house; from that position someone may have seen the faint outline of my crouched figure against an angle of lighted pane. If Stoltz employed guards in his grounds I was in for a rough time because there might be more than one; I was unarmed; and I didn't know the terrain at all out here.

If they didn't take me out they'd soon run me to ground and drag me in front of Stoltz. In which case I'd blown everything. There were two other possibilities. I left those for a little later. I was still rolling and I was in the shelter of some bushes on the far side of the lawn now. I paused to get my breath, conscious of the heavy thumping of my heart in my chest.

You're getting old, Mike, I told myself. That's another thing I always say on every case. But it's something that comes to mind when one's thirty-three and the reflexes begin to slow down. I gave myself a twisted grin in the darkness and the rising wind that was making a shadowy death trap of the grounds where every trembling of foliage could have concealed my marksman.

He'd used a pistol with a silencer; which might be significant and led me back to my two possibilities. The shot could still have been fired by someone in Stoltz' employ, but merely intended as a warning. Or could someone else be watching Kettle's partner out here for some purposes of his own. The more I thought about it the more I thought it likely.

In which case things might be a little more complex than I figured. I was wriggling slowly backward into the bushes, trying not to make too much noise. I hadn't seen or heard anything of the hit-man since the slug had sliced the tree but that didn't mean to say he wasn't still around. The house was clearly in sight, the French windows shining blandly through the darkness.

I was backing away again when I saw a fleeting silhouette briefly pause in front of the end window as though someone were peering in: then the shadow disappeared. But I knew he was going back down toward the front entrance because I could hear the very faint grit of a shoe on the flagstones.

I was in control again now. I got out the bushes, on to grass the other side, and straightened up. Then I went fast across the lawn, still keeping the screen of foliage between me and the man with the pistol. The moisture was pattering heavily from the leaves of the trees, masking my movements across the grass. Fast as I was, the other man was faster.

I was about halfway across the darkness between the house and the road when I saw someone going away at speed down the big alley in front of the mansion. I got up there as quickly as I could, trying not to make any noise. I was still about a hundred feet away when he gained the main entrance. There was some light coming in from the street lamps in the lane outside.

I caught only a glimpse but it was a tall man in a light-coloured raincoat with a dark fedora pulled down over his eyes; his face was screened by the turned-up collar, the hands thrust deep into the pockets of the coat. I was still a few yards from the entrance when I heard a car gun up. I reached the sidewalk in time to see the dim rear-lights going down the lane at speed.

The low sport-job went away at quite a lick then, the howl of the engine showing there was a lot of power under the bonnet. I didn't bother to get to the Buick; I knew I wouldn't stand a chance against that thing. And I hadn't been able to read the licence plate.

I got back in the driving seat of the Buick, set fire to a cigarette and pasted my damp thoughts together. I had quite a few things to think about on the drive home.

The bulk of the Smith-Wesson in its nylon harness made a comforting pressure against my chest muscles as I leaned back in my swivel chair, following Stella's brisk movements as she went from her typewriter to the filing cabinet and then over to the brewing-up alcove.

Though it had started fine it was raining again this morning and slivers of what looked like sleet were scarring the window and dribbling down the panes to make long smears of the dirt and grit that the smog deposited on the glass.

Stella paused in her soothing ministrations among the coffee cups and came back to sit on the edge of my desk to swing a long leg tantalisingly.

'So what was this character doing up there, Mike?'

'I was hoping you'd tell me,' I said.

Stella smiled briefly. I could have watched it all morning. Instead, I switched to the cracks in the ceiling. Things were safer that way.

'Opposition or rival?'

I gave her a grudging look.

'It took me half an hour to arrive at those conclusions. Lay out some lines of reasoning for me.'

Stella's smile lasted her all the way to the alcove. She fussed around a while longer and then went back to her desk. She brought me over a sheaf of mail to sign.

'Mr Stellenbosch was on earlier. He wanted to know if you had any line on his daughter.'

I sighed.

'I was afraid you were going to say that. She was last heard of up in the San Fernando Valley.'

I met Stella's level gaze.

'Helping to run a riding stable. The story I hear is that the old guy isn't her father but her step-father. And after what happened between them if she never sees him again it'll be too soon.'

Stella puckered her lips in a noiseless whistle.

'Like that, is it?'

I nodded.

'Just like that.'

Stella folded her arms across her full breasts and put her head on one side.

'So what do I tell him?'

'Be diplomatic,' I told her. 'I already used up more than his minimal fee on the foot-work.'

Stella's eyes were very bright now.

'And you promised the girl you wouldn't tell,' she said softly.

'That's about it, honey.'

I was saved further interrogation by the

74

buzzing of the percolator. I went through the sheaf of stuff, checking it out and signing where necessary. Like always, it was immaculate. I put the bundle on the other side of the desk in the end and sat staring into the depths of the cup Stella had put down on my blotter.

I could taste the beans long before I nuzzled into the contents. I added a mite more sugar and sat back, my eyes half-closed. That isn't very difficult at the best of times. This morning I felt beat, even though I hadn't even started the day.

Stella was seated in the client's chair opposite, her pink-nailed hands embracing her cup.

'Item,' she said. 'Stoltz has tried to kill his partner on a number of occasions. Brake incident confirmed by garage. Several other incidents on the yellow list corroborated by Elizabeth Goddard, who was present on at least one occasion.'

'You do a great précis,' I said.

Stella lifted her eyes from her cup and shot me a swift glance.

'You want my help or not?'

'Who's arguing?' I said. 'I was just agreeing with you.'

Stella took a delicate sip at her coffee, reached out for the biscuit tin that was lying in the centre of the desk between us.

'Somewhat ill-advisedly you're on private

property, snooping around Stoltz' house when someone takes a shot at you with a silenced weapon.'

'I don't agree with the first part but it's accurate as far as it goes,' I said.

Stella gave me an incredulous look.

'We'll argue about the first part later. And you were fortunate the hit-man wasn't accurate under the circumstances.'

'I won't quarrel with that,' I told her.

Stella took a deep breath and plunged on.

'We have three possibles here. We can rule out guards in the grounds because the character wouldn't have taken off like that.'

'That's what I figured.'

Stella frowned as she gazed at the blotter like she could see pictures there that were hidden from me.

'Then maybe somebody else is interested in Stoltz and his girl-friend.'

I stared at her without saying anything. It paid off because she went on without pausing.

'It could be his way of warning you off.'

I kept my eyes down on my coffee cup this time.

'Or somebody doesn't like you.'

I could feel Stella's eyes fixed on my face.

'It's an interesting theory, honey, but why? I could think of dozens of people who don't like me and for very good reasons. But why would they want to choose a moment when I'm on a case and observing a suspect?'

Stella smiled faintly.

'I'm just putting up a few clay-pigeons for you to shoot down. That shot was a warning. If he'd wanted to the gunman could have taken you out. And he probably saw you cross to the bushes. Yet he didn't shoot again. Why?'

I took another swig of the coffee.

'Some good questions. You have a point though. It opens up some interesting possibilities.'

Stella put her cup down, the sharp, brittle sound cutting through the faint hum of stalled traffic on the boulevard outside.

'That's what I'm here for, Mike.'

I leaned back in my chair.

'So that's the reason. I thought it was to provide some decorative relief between the filing cabinet and the fan.'

Stella's eyes flashed and her voice was deceptively calm.

'You want some more coffee? In the cup or on your suit?'

I grinned.

'Let's call a truce. I'd like to hear more of your ideas.'

This time Stella's smile lasted her all the way to the alcove and back.

CHAPTER NINE

1

The rain had stopped when I reached the Dittmar Building, and there were few people in the lobby as I got in the elevator and buttoned my way up to the fourth floor. My operation was of little more practical use than last night's foray out at The Grange but I needed to earn some of Kettle's money and I had to start somewhere.

If I couldn't approach Stoltz direct I could only keep his activities under observation and hope that something would break to give me a lead. The estates division of Cesarwich was a similar lay-out to that on the floor above except that this suite was situated at the far end of the corridor.

I went on past the frosted glass panelling with the gold stencilled lettering, listening to the faint abrasive patter of typewriters and still kicking a few ideas around. None of them made sense. But then they never do until a case is seventy per cent through. Sometimes later than that. Especially on my sort of assignment.

There was a staircase leading down at the far end, round a right-angle turn. The plushly carpeted corridor gave out on to bare concrete round the angle. I went down the stairs lightly, two treads at a time, pausing on each landing. Like I figured it was a fire exit; it didn't say so but I must have missed the notices somewhere; later I found they were outside in the corridors on the different floors.

They gave out in the end on the ground floor, the main double doors, lightly secured with a self-locking bar, leading to the sidewalk. I lit a cigarette, putting the spent match-stalk in the box and went slowly back up again. When I got to the fourth floor I stayed on the landing, finishing my cigarette, keeping watch on the corridor leading to Stoltz' office.

It looked like being a long wait but time was something I had plenty of on this case. For a day or two at any rate. Elizabeth Goddard was convinced Harry Kettle's luck was running out; and he'd certainly seemed a much frightened man. But a week ought to give me enough leeway to come up with something.

There was no pattern emerging at the moment. And it would need an accountant to sort through the company's books to see what was wrong, if anything. I was uneasy with the contract, had been from the beginning, and I felt badly out of my depth. That feeling was always uppermost at the start of a case and it persists until one can make some sense of apparently disconnected events.

Kettle was clear in his own mind about what was going on; I was far from clear in my own.

Stoltz' motive was apparently buried in masses of figures and company reports and even the courts, using trained accountants and experts in company law sometimes took months to sort such things out.

I stayed on in the corridor for more than an hour, smoking three cigarettes; putting the stubs back in the package; and teasing out the tangled ends of my ragged thoughts. I was conscious of figures passing to and fro in the corridor beyond and I snapped to attention as soon as anyone showed at the entrance to Cesarwich' office. I didn't see anyone I knew; anything suspicious; and certainly not Stoltz or his girl-friend.

I figured I would know them if I saw them again. What I was really waiting for was a tall man in a light raincoat wearing a dark fedora but that sort of thing happened only in movies. In the meantime I was well-placed in here, out of sight; fairly comfortable; and I could hear if anyone came up the stairway long before they got here.

Similarly, if anyone came toward my doorway I had only to push my way through into the corridor as though I'd just come up from a lower floor on some perfectly legitimate errand. There was no problem about that; the only reason I was lurking here was because I didn't want to blow my cover and it would look ridiculous if I leaned against the wall in the public corridor leading to the offices.

I gave another glance at my watch. It was an hour and a half now. About par for the course. I stubbed out the butt of my last cigarette on the carton and put it back in the foil. I never leave any evidence of my presence around. It's too easy to read; especially for trained police officers.

And I'd known too many horror stories of private investigators who'd left traces of their presence in murder apartments and found themselves entangled in compromising situations. I was too keen on retaining my licence to fall into that trap. Then I heard the heavy vibration of footsteps over the carpeting in the corridor beyond. They were confident, purposeful footsteps, totally unlike those I'd been hearing all morning.

I was still putting the package back into my pocket, the weight of the Smith-Wesson pressing against my chest muscles, and it took me another second or two to get to the small glass window in the door leading to the corridor. I was just too late for a full-face view of the big man who was opening the main door to Cesarwich Enterprises. He was about six feet tall and wore a neat, well-pressed dark suit like a business executive.

He also wore a dark matching derby which was a little unusual in L.A. His face was turned away from me so that was about all I made out. His black shoes were highly polished and as he turned into the doorway I could see he had an expensive pigskin valise in his unoccupied hand, which was attached to his wrist by a steel bracelet and chain like diplomatic and security personnel wear. His wrist was very dark and hairy and also bore an expensive-looking gold watch.

I stood and watched the door close silently behind him. I stayed glued to the small window in the upper half of the door, only moving back whenever anyone passed up and down the corridor. I must have stayed there for more than half an hour. There had been something vaguely familiar about the character in the dark suit and I wanted to make sure I glimpsed his face next time.

The door was opening slowly now. My man was backing out. I got closer to the panel. He was obviously talking to someone inside the office. He had his left hand on the door handle and I then saw that the pigskin case was no longer attached to his wrist. He had apparently delivered something valuable to Cesarwich. He finished at last and backed away, turning to close the door.

I had a clear view of his face now. It was a hard, durable one that looked incongruous below the staid derby. The eyes were cold like those of a snake and the thin, straight lips drawn back in a wolfish smile revealed square white teeth, beneath the heavy black mustache.

It was a familiar face too. I had the character pegged. He was a man called Angelo Pacelli, well-known in gangland circles. He was officially listed as a fruit importer. What most people didn't know, and what the L.A. police knew but could never make stick, was that his most profitable occupation was that of a professional hit-man.

As he'd just visited Herman Stoltz that interested me a good deal. I was taking the stairs to the street two at a time before he had reached the end of the corridor.

2

I got back in the Buick and had the engine running quietly before my man showed. It was starting to spit with rain again now and I put the wipers on to clear the screen. The jaded-looking bronze fountain was switched off today, perhaps to avoid competing with the weather. My heap was down the far end of the concourse, under the trees; there were a lot of automobiles parked in here and I didn't think I'd been spotted.

Pacelli was coming down the main steps to the concourse; I dropped below window level in the driving seat and waited until he'd gone on to a stone-coloured Studebaker parked about a hundred yards farther off. I could see his exhaust smoke now and I eased the Buick out, waiting for Pacelli to slot into the traffic flow.

I dropped in two cars behind and started following as he began making time in an eastward direction across town. I made a note of his licence number and jotted it on the scratch-pad I keep on the dashboard shelf as I drove with one hand. The traffic was fairly heavy and I kept my eyes peeled at the intersections as there were some complicated turn-offs in this section.

The rain was coming down still more heavily and I moved up at the first opportunity, keeping one car between us. The man driving the stone-coloured Studebaker wouldn't know he was being followed but Pacelli was a professional and there wouldn't be any allowance for mistakes. I was interested in finding out if Stoltz had any more underworld links.

The hit-man had just visited him, possibly to deliver cash; what I wanted to know was who had sent him. Then I might begin to make some sense out of this tangle. I changed down and drifted up to another set of lights, waiting for them to change. Pacelli had his indicator going now. He was headed left, down the next intersecting boulevard and I signalled too, easing over toward the offside lane.

A big, red-faced truckie with an angry expression started leaning on his horn until I gave him one of my best smiles. He didn't know what to make of that; it put him off. People in L.A. aren't used to politeness. I grinned in the mirror as the big snout of his truck drew back, leaving me a slot to get through. Pacelli was already gunning up rapidly.

I gave the truckie an acknowledgment signal with my hand for his courtesy; his pleasure in the rear view mirror followed me all the way down the boulevard. The big Studebaker was eating up the blocks, and I put my toe down to follow, hoping nothing would bore in from an intersection. There were more lights another couple of blocks ahead and I eased back, leaving three automobiles between as Pacelli drew up.

He was second in the queue so I knew he wouldn't be very fast away from the lights. I was ready for him now but I was still convinced he didn't know I was following; there was no reason for him to suspect. If my hunch was correct he'd just been carrying out a routine drop.

We carried on down the boulevard, still going in a vaguely eastward direction. The better locations were petering out and we were in a section of vacant lots, warehouses and development of the tin shack variety, where various light industries were carrying on business. There were still two cars between when the Studebaker signalled right and turned off into a puddled concrete forecourt.

I pulled the Buick up in front of the garish neon of a hamburger joint and killed the motor, keeping the wipers going for a little while longer. Pacelli evidently intended to stay because I heard his motor cut out and the rear stop lights went off. A moment later I heard the slam of the driving door and he got out, his head bowed under the slanting rain.

He went off across the forecourt toward a group of warehouses where fruit trucks were drawn up in a sheeted cluster, looking straight in front of him. I reached for my raincoat and pulled it over my shoulders before getting out the Buick. I slammed the door behind me and sprinted across the pavement to the shelter of an awning in front of the hamburger joint.

The windows were so misted and steamed I couldn't make out much of the interior. I put the raincoat on and buttoned it. Pacelli had disappeared by now. I walked on down toward the forecourt I wanted, and went on over toward the fruit warehouses, ignoring the Studebaker, my head bowed beneath the slashing rain.

Seemed like I ought to invest in an umbrella if this case kept up. I gave myself a strained grin. It was all I had for humour at the moment and I intended to make the most of it. The place was called Amoco Fruit Importers Inc., and Pacelli had gone into a long alleyway between two gaunt sheds that cast heavy shadow across the wet concrete.

There was no-one in the immediate vicinity and I figured there wouldn't be much interest in someone like me walking purposefully across, presumably to visit an office in rear of the buildings. I could see a faded notice screwed to the sheet metal wall of one of the sheds that the cement path did in fact lead to offices and stores.

I went on down, my footsteps muffled in the falling rain, the bulk of the Smith-Wesson reassuring against the tautness of my raincoat. I could see the whole length of the path and there was nothing moving in the pale yellow ribbon beneath the rain. I got about a quarter of the way along and found, at the end of the first building, there were more paths debouching to the right.

Large wooden packing cases made aisles at the rear of the building and I could hear the faint whine of a fork-lift truck operating somewhere. It was darker in here and I slackened for a moment, keeping my eyes on the path ahead. That was my biggest mistake.

I had just got past the first packing case when something stirred in the shadow. I had only half-turned, my fingers nowhere near the Smith-Wesson before someone clamped down a security blackout. I went out like vaudeville.

CHAPTER TEN

1

There was rain on my face and something rough too. As I opened my eyes the latter resolved itself into the tousled face of a large, friendly-looking dog. It was his tongue which had been exploring my features. I put my hand up into the reassuring mass of his damp fur.

'Great,' I said.

The dog gave a delighted snuffle, wagged its tail enthusiastically and licked my face again. I rolled over, conscious of a stabbing pain at the back of my skull. Recollection returned. I was still lying where I'd been sapped, in rear of the fruit warehouse. It was the oldest trick in the world. Pacelli hadn't been fooled from the first. He'd just led me here to ditch me while he went about his business.

Whatever that was. Which opened up some interesting possibilities. I knew I had all the time in the world now. And the danger had passed. With a character like Pacelli I'd have been outed or dead straight off. So he didn't want me dead. I got up, leaning drunkenly against the packing case, while the dog fussed around my feet. I hadn't been searched because my wallet and all the other stuff in my pockets was intact.

And I'd been out only a few minutes because my clothing was merely slightly wet. I'd been lying in the shelter of the case, of course, but I'd have been drenched if I'd been out an hour or more. I checked by my watch, having some difficulty in focusing. I made it not much more than ten minutes.

The dog was still getting excited so I leaned down and patted him absently. That seemed to please him more than ever. I knew without looking that the Smith-Wesson was still there. I had trouble in standing so I found a smaller packing case that I could sit on and slumped down, my head in my hands. I would have looked very peculiar had there been anyone to see but the place was deserted.

Which was no doubt why Pacelli had chosen it. The dog was quiet now. It nuzzled its wet nose sympathetically against my fingers. I got up then, found I could stand properly. I took two tottering steps, the rain refreshing on my face and felt a whole lot better. The dog ambled happily at my side as I went on back down the cement path, trying to look as casual and normal as possible.

I knew the back of my raincoat was probably plastered with mud and the inside of my head was exploding rhythmically, but I didn't want to reach up to touch the place in case my head fell off. The dog seemed perfectly happy, confident that it had saved my life and as we got back out on to the forecourt it wagged its tail once more, put another streak of dirt on my trousers with its forepaws and trotted forward obediently to where a big truckie in a mackinaw jacket waited for it.

It jumped obediently up into the passenger seat of the truck, still with the superior smile on its face. The truckie didn't say anything or stare at me so I guessed I looked fairly normal. I've noticed that before after similar incidents. The damage is mostly subjective; an earthquake to the victim but a mere hiccup to the passer-by. You're getting quite a philosopher, Mike, I told myself.

I went on down the sidewalk, the rain stinging my eyelids, feeling like I was treading on scrambled eggs. Somehow I got in the Buick and slumped behind the wheel. I closed my eyes and must have passed out. When I again became aware of rain streaking the windshield, I found another twenty minutes had passed. But I felt better then. After another year or so I felt I might live with a little kindness and gentle treatment. I let the gear in very cautiously and crawled away from there.

2

Stella's face looked concerned. She leaned over the desk and probed my scalp with gentle fingers. Then she took a clean handkerchief, poured something on to it from a bottle with a red label. I smelt a pungent perfume and then felt a stinging sensation. Stella made a soothing noise and moved away.

'You'll live,' she said gently.

'Thanks,' I told her. 'With a little kindness.'

'Which includes coffee, I take it?'

'It would help,' I said.

Stella smiled and went back over toward the alcove. She came back and cleared her surgical kit before going to sit on a corner of the desk. I sat and frowned at the window. The rain showed no sign of letting up.

'You think this character was the same man who shot at you out at Stoltz', Mike?'

'Not necessarily,' I said. 'We could have two separate sets of people.'

Stella put her head on one side and frowned at me reflectively.

'In which case it could be getting complicated.'

'It is already,' I said. 'I've been thinking things over on my way in. Even Pacelli may not have hit me. Supposing someone saw me following him and waited behind that crate?'

Stella shrugged, the frown still on her face.

'It's your case, Mike,' she said helpfully.

She went back to the alcove while I listened to the little men beating tattoos on the inside of my skull with their iron slicing bars. They were getting fainter now. After a cup of coffee and an hour wearing out my pants on the seat of my swivel chair I'd be almost as good as new.

Presently Stella put the coffee down on the desk and went around to sit in the client's chair. It was just after lunch and we hadn't been disturbed. Not that I expected a spate of cases, especially in this weather.

'We know a few things,' she said presently.

'Sure,' I said. 'Kettle thinks Stoltz is threatening his life. And Stoltz is mixed up with a known hit-man.'

'Who now knows you're on to him,' Stella said.

'If it was Pacelli who hit me,' I told her.

I went on gloomily stirring my coffee. Then I took the first sips and felt a little better.

'Knowing Pacelli's reputation he could have hit me harder,' I said.

Stella shivered a little despite the warmth of the room. She said nothing so I went on.

'A skilled man sapped me. He put just enough pressure on to take me out for a quarter of an hour. But was he with Pacelli? If Pacelli had spotted me tailing him he might or might not have known me.'

Stella arched her eyebrows.

'Meaning?'

'Meaning that he would probably have gone through my wallet to establish my identity.'

'You have a nice list of questions, Mike,' Stella said brightly.

I grunted and nuzzled into the coffee again.

'And precious few answers.'

Stella pushed her chair back from the desk and cupped her hands round one smooth, sun-tanned knee.

'There is another possibility, Mike.'

'Hundreds,' I said.

Stella gave the refined little noise which passes for a snort with her.

'I'm talking about plausible hypotheses.'

'My, we are getting fancy,' I said.

There were little spots of red burning on her cheeks now. I lit a cigarette and put the spent match-stalk into the earthenware tray. I blew out tendrils of smoke which danced in the warm air before fading imperceptibly.

'I'm still waiting.'

'Supposing Pacelli was on his way to report to someone. In some distant building farther down that concrete path.'

'I'm with you,' I said.

Stella had a pained look on her face now.

'Someone else was watching from the fruit warehouse fronting the forecourt, maybe. In an office over the top, perhaps. Someone who realised you shouldn't have been there.'

Stella paused for my interruption but I didn't oblige her this time. She looked almost disappointed.

'He just had time to run down, pick up something heavy and wait behind that crate.'

'Sounds plausible,' I said.

'That's it,' Stella said.

93

'He went off to fetch Pacelli. Either he couldn't find him easily or he took too long. In the meantime you recovered consciousness and left.'

I looked at her grudgingly.

'You may have something, honey.'

'There's one way of finding out,' she said.

A sudden stab of pain on the top of my head stopped my next question. I held out my coffee cup for a refill. Stella went off and was back again so quickly I hardly had time to close my eyes. I added a little more sugar and burrowed my way into the second cup. Stella sat watching with that marvellous patience of hers.

'You think I ought to check out the offices in back of the warehouse?' I said. 'Preferably tonight.'

Stella shrugged.

'Depends how you feel, Mike. But it could be a lead.'

I grinned.

'Looks like I'm in the fruit business,' I said.

I started to work my way through to the bottom of the cup.

CHAPTER ELEVEN

1

The weather was marginally better tonight. Leastways, compared to when I was out at Stoltz' house. This time it was only like Reel 8 of *The Rains Came*. The sequence where Nigel Bruce gets washed away in the middle of a sour tirade. I parked the car a couple of blocks down and gum-shoed back along the façades of the buildings, keeping in doorways and under the shelter of awnings as much as possible.

I stopped some way before I got to Amoco Fruit Importers. I could still feel my head faintly throbbing. The bump was coming up a treat. I had no wish to repeat the performance. I was in a darkened doorway now, which belonged to someone with a retarded childhood because the window was filled with hundreds of battered lead soldiers.

I could make that out by the glare of neon coming from the opposite sidewalk. I got well back, took the Smith-Wesson out my shoulder holster, checked the safety and put it in my right-hand raincoat pocket. I wasn't looking for any rough stuff tonight but at least I was a little better prepared.

I eased out under the awning. It was about

two hundred yards up to the warehouse forecourt. Trouble was it was full of light. And I could hear the heavy throbbing of trucks and see the flash of headlights as the big refrigerated fruit containers pulled in and out. Both Stella and I had forgotten that people in that line of business do a lot of their work at night.

There had to be an easier way. There was no point in taking the same route as my last visit. Not unless I wanted something even more drastic to happen. There was an alley on the right just ahead, beyond the parade of shops where I was holed up. I'd noticed it yesterday. It wouldn't do any harm to see where it went.

I turned up my coat-collar and went on down, the rain cool and refreshing on my face. I stepped into the alley without hesitating, the butt of the Smith-Wesson cool cold on my fingers. There was no-one about on the sidewalks in this section but it's always best to be decisive. There's nothing so suspicious as a character who hangs around a street corner on a dark night. You should know, Faraday, I told myself.

I was in the darkness now, my eyes adjusted to the lowered intensity of the lighting. There were a lot of puddles on the unmade, cindered pathway in here and I aimed to avoid most of them. My progress was noisier than I would have liked but the throbbing of the diesels helped to cover my movements.

There were lights set atop steel poles in the next section and I found my way along the perimeter of a heavy chain-link fence which bordered the used-car lot. There were some torches bobbing about in the middle like a few seedy characters were inspecting late-night purchases. Or some small-time grifters wiring up a jalopy for a quick getaway. It was no business of mine; I had enough trouble at the moment.

I could see the fruit warehouses now, silhouetted against the glare of the lights; there were two sets of buildings between, as well as the used-car lot so I was all right for the time being. I would have to take extra care only when I got on private property. Assuming I could reach the warehouses from here. It would be my luck to find a stream or a railroad cutting running between.

The rain had eased a little and the going wasn't so unpleasant as I figured. I was almost at the end of the lot; there was no-one around and to my right was nothing but the blank brick wall of something that looked like more warehousing and loading bays. The business, whatever it was, couldn't have been night-intensive, because everything was shut up and deserted.

The chain-link was giving out and when I'd skirted a couple of large and deep pools of rainwater I found I'd come out in a cross-section. The cinder path continued in rear of the buildings and cut right across, making a T-junction. The walkway continued right at an oblique angle and probably came out on the sidewalk somewhere near where I'd left my heap.

It went on to the left and must eventually tie up with the rear of the fruit warehouses, probably linking with the concrete path I'd already been down. I was making no attempt at concealment now; from all I'd noted I figured I was on a public path and I'd act on that assumption until I got closer.

A minute later I was in rear of the Amoco operation where all the rumpus was still going on. The path gave out at this point in a wilderness of old timber and oil drums. Beyond was nothing but scrubland, waving grass and another chain-link fence, making a cul-de-sac. At my left, in rear of the premises I wanted was a steel-framed gate set into the fencing. It was locked, like I figured.

I went back down to the end of the cul-de-sac. I found an empty oil drum and rolled it back, making as little noise as possible. It was early evening and I had plenty of time. This was all I intended to do for Kettle's money tonight. The tap on the head had already used up some of his credit. I had trouble getting the drum up but I balanced it on top of the wire in the end. I waited until a couple of trucks were revving up and let it go; it landed on soft earth with an almost inaudible noise. I went back and hunted out another drum which was also empty.

Then I had stepped up on to the metal angle bracket at the top of the fence and jumped down the other side. I rolled the second drum into deeper shadow on my side of the fence. I'd use it to get out later. With all the lights in front I hadn't a hope of leaving unnoticed that way. My heart was pumping evenly and gently as I found a ribbon of concrete that led me back toward the dark, silent bulk of the buildings I wanted.

2

It was a process of elimination and it took me longer than I figured. Some of the places were obvious warehouses; others storage buildings and single-storey metal sheds. There were only three that looked anything like offices. Two of them had metal plates screwed alongside the doorways. I risked my pencil flash to identify them. One was the registered office of a plant-hire contractor; another, surprisingly, the business address of an aircraft crop-spraying operation.

The third, connected direct to the concrete path on which I'd been slugged was a substantial concrete building, painted cream and with smart-looking plastic sun-blinds at the windows. The path went round to the rear of the building and at an angle to the front was an entrance porch. That had both inner and outer doors so I didn't waste my time there; I wouldn't have even if I hadn't spotted the burglar alarm system in its metal box atop the building.

The white-painted board said: CHILTERN STATIONERY SUPPLIES. My spirits sank a little. Not that I'd expected much. Maybe Pacelli had me spotted and had merely led me literally up the concrete path, his destination somewhere entirely different. And then again maybe he hadn't.

I went round in rear and examined a feature I'd already noticed. It had been a very close, humid day; places like this most probably wouldn't have air-conditioning. And perhaps the little lady who did the typing and answered the phone here had been careless.

She'd closed and locked all the big windows that fronted the office but hadn't noticed the half-light which stood ajar, only half visible in the shadow; held open by the small metal bar and its retaining pin. I checked around with the flash, made sure there was no alarm connected to the framework.

I was getting all the breaks tonight. I found a plastic dustbin and carried it over quietly and carefully. I was sweating a little now. It was almost too smooth. I was carrying out a felony, of course; and if I got too careless I'd maybe run into one of the boys in blue who might just choose tonight to come around in rear of the warehouses with his flashlight.

I caught the rictus of my smile in the dark pane of the nearest window. I was up on top of the bin now. From there it was only a short step to the sill.

I lifted the window and had wriggled over inside in a minute, making sure I didn't lose any buttons off my raincoat. I'd leave wet footmarks on the linoleum but that couldn't be helped. And I'd rub them out before I left.

I closed the window behind me and dropped the blind. I stood in the semi-darkness, smelling the stale warm smell that offices have; compounded of dust; old coffee grounds; and the pungent aroma of that stuff they use to clean typewriters with; and the chemical that blots out the mistakes on the manager's letters. I was talking like an editorial out of the Businessman's Friend. I moved away from the window, getting the outlines of the furniture now.

What I wanted was the manager's office. It wasn't locked. The furniture was simple stuff; the sort of metal desk, filing cabinet and uncomfortable chairs that are turned out by the million and sold the length and breadth of the States. I padded around, being careful where I put my moist fingers. I sat down behind the desk in the end, making sure I had my handkerchief ready to clean every surface

I'd touched.

It was pretty dark in here but there was a little light spilling in through the windows. I went on over and closed the only blind that was open. It would be sheer carelessness now if I was discovered by some night man on his rounds. Most sites like this had watchmen retained jointly by a number of companies. That way it cut the cost.

I found my way back to the desk and sat down. I got my pencil-flash and holding it low went across the drawers. There was a key in the lock of the central drawer like the owner had left in a hurry. I went quickly down the rest, found they were all unlocked. It took me a little while to go through the stuff.

I didn't really know what I was looking for but that wasn't out of the ordinary for me. There was a lot of stuff in the middle drawer, including invoices for stationery, business letters and material of such increasing banality that I almost dozed off once or twice. But not quite. When I'd finished with the first drawer I made sure all the stuff was as I'd found it, left the key at the same angle and dusted off the handle.

I went down the rest of the drawers, one by one, working methodically through. The result was the same in each case. Nothing but routine material relating to a fairly large wholesale stationery business. There was nothing personal; nothing out of the ordinary; and certainly nothing to link Pacelli or Stoltz with this set-up. I began to feel I'd made a mistake.

But I'm nothing if not persistent. I glanced at my watch. Already I'd been in here twenty minutes. It was hardly likely anyone would come back tonight but I didn't want to hang it out. It was then I heard a boot scrape on the concrete path outside the main entrance. I already had the pencil-flash off. I sat on at the desk, feeling sweat trickling down my shirt-band, listening to the lonely pumping of my heart in my chest.

A fly buzzed ominously in the stillness. Then I heard a rattling sound as someone tried the front door. I could see a gleam of light, coming in momentarily underneath the door leading to the office I was in. It led off the entrance and someone was shining the light in through the glass doors. I sat still for another year.

Then the footsteps shifted away. There was another long silence. The fly buzzed again. I wondered for a moment if I'd remembered to shut the window. It was obviously the night man on his rounds. If he went round in back to check the windows it was equally obvious he'd spot the plastic dustbin. Whether he would guess there was someone inside was another matter. Maybe not. I waited another year. Then I heard the footsteps again, farther off now. I relaxed and again turned to the desk.

There was one place I hadn't looked; not

that I expected to find anything now. But I might as well do the job properly while I was here. The desk had a sort of console at the back of it; a set of shelves which rose from the surface about a foot. They were made of metal too and probably screwed to the surface. I tentatively felt them and found they were an integral part of the desk like I figured.

There were two largish drawers, neither of them locked. I slid open the first. At the top was a bundle of bills done up with an elastic band. There was about three or four thousand dollars' worth there. But what riveted me was the slip of paper stapled to the edge of the bundle. It had Pacelli written on it in wavy writing, in very faint pencil.

The whole place seemed transformed. Though there still wasn't any sense in Kettle's tangle I had a feeling that there was a process involved that would add up if I worked at it. I went through the two drawers quickly. I had struck gold. There was a lot of guarded correspondence between Stoltz and Pacelli.

It was pretty innocuous, typed stuff, but it could have meant something to the initiated; the clipped, enigmatic sentences might have been a simple form of coded instruction. All the letters to Pacelli were on Cesarwich headed notepaper and the envelopes postmarked L.A.; Stoltz hadn't signed them but each letter bore the carelessly scribbled initials, H.S. That added up too.

Where there were envelopes they were addressed to Pacelli c/o Chiltern Stationery Supplies office. I guessed it was merely a letter drop. The people here wouldn't know anything but the secretary would merely pass on correspondence and cash. The whole thing must have seemed so open that the drawers weren't even locked.

Then I remembered that maybe the manager or the secretary would need to place cash for Pacelli in the drawers. It was a simple but effective arrangement and the more I thought about it the more I liked it.

I went through everything again but on the face of it it was nothing but an innocuous business correspondence. There was little else for me here but I had established the necessary link. I spent the next ten minutes putting everything back as I'd found it. I was streaming with sweat by this time. It seemed remarkably hot in here. But then it would be with no fans going and the windows closed and the blinds drawn.

I could still hear the soft, insistent patter of rain at the windows. That could cover the distant sound of the night man's footsteps and I would have to watch it. I went over the desk again, carefully erasing any possible finger-prints and any visible trace of my presence there. I adjusted the swivel chair to the same angle as I'd found it and went around the place for the last time, checking detail with the pocket-flash.

When I was satisfied it would need Father Brown to dig up any trace of my presence I padded into the outer office, switching off the pencil-flash and putting it back in my pocket. I racked up the slats of the blind a little and peeked through. Rain kept on streaking the glass and it took me a little while to make out the detail.

I had the top window latched back and was alert to the slightest sound. When I was a hundred per cent certain there was no-one around I went over the floor, obliterating any traces of my wet foot-prints with a duster I found on top of a cupboard. They had dried out fairly well by this time but there was no point in advertising my presence.

Then I went out the way I'd come in; I had a bad moment or two, easing across the metal bar in the top window but I made it in the end without putting one of my size nines through the main sheet. I got my balance on the sill at last and reached in to put the top latching bar back in the same position so that the window remained three inches open as I'd found it.

It took only a few seconds more to replace the dustbin. I was getting nice and damp by this time so I didn't hang around too long. Nothing moved in all the wide stretch of the cement path but the heavy throbbing of the fruit lorries went on as they revved in and out the Amoco forecourt. I had to leave the oil drum in situ when I got back over the fence but I hoped no-one would notice.

I dropped down and replaced the other oil drum with the junk at the end of the cul-de-sac. I got back to the T-junction, turned left this time, away from the lights and re-joined the main stem a couple of hundred yards farther down. I slid behind the wheel of the Buick, set fire to a cigarette, looking at my dark, sardonic features in the rear mirror by the flare of the match.

Then I stopped kicking my brains out and started making time toward Park West.

CHAPTER TWELVE

1

It was sunny this morning with that clear, well-scrubbed look L.A. sometimes wears before the heat of the day has toasted the sidewalks. I'd got out early, after giving Stella a ring before she left for the office. I made it to The Grange just before nine o'clock and slotted the Buick in alongside the shade of a flowering hedge, where I wouldn't look too obtrusive.

My head had mended nicely now but I was missing Stella's coffee. Even the cracks in the office ceiling seemed attractive compared to what might turn out to be another abortive assignment. I'd seemed to spend all my time on the case in stake-out so far. Or had I already said that? It was getting too warm to bother.

All I could see was the drive, with the lodge next to it and the gates still hooked back. I sat for a few minutes and whiled away the time with a radio bulletin switched on low. I was still sitting there, thinking of nothing in particular, when a glittering white Rolls drifted down the driveway and pulled up quietly in front of the lodge.

The horn gave a discreet fanfaronade and a tall, hard-looking man in a brown windbreaker came out the lodge. I looked him over carefully but he hadn't got the build of the character who'd shot at me the other night. I was pretty certain of that. The driving window had slid down now and Stoltz was talking to the gateman.

I could see it was Stoltz because although he was sitting on the side farthest away from me a beam of sunshine illuminated the interior of the big vehicle and I caught again the aristocratic profile with the blond hair and the clipped black mustache. He was wearing a smart blue blazer with a white silk shirt and striped tie this morning and he looked like Patric Knowles on his day off.

Presently he finished giving his instructions to the man in the windbreaker and I could see a feather of dark blue smoke coming out the

Rolls exhaust. I started my own engine as the huge white machine cruised forward, the sunlight sparking on the distinctive radiator grille and the silver lady on the bonnet.

I knew he'd be going in toward the city so I followed at leisure, making sure I kept him in sight; that wasn't too difficult because the white body-work showed up miles ahead. It was one of the most frustrating and boring mornings of my life. He drove first to a sports-good store on one of the main boulevards; he took up the last slot in a railed-off enclosure and I had to circle the block and almost missed him coming away.

It was around ten by this time. He next went to the Dittmar Building, presumably to his own office; it was too risky to follow him in there and pointless besides so I parked my heap and went for a quick coffee at a place almost opposite, where I could keep a look-out and maybe do a minute mile if I could get back across the traffic flow in time.

I had an hour to wait when I got to the Buick so I filled it in with a crossword I found in a magazine Stella had left on the back seat. It was dated the previous spring so it shows how often Stella travels with me. The clues were puerile and my answers problematical so I wasn't too unhappy when Stoltz reappeared.

He was still alone. It was around twelve by this time and it had been a great morning for non-incidents. We drove for an hour, up into the foothills. Traffic was light but I kept a few other vehicles between us. It was cooler up here and I was grateful for the breeze that came in through the driving window. Mount Baldy, in the far distance, still had a powdering of snow and far below the Pacific was a deep mauve colour close in, shading to pale green farther out.

I could see the white wake of a coaster like an arrow-head carved in the water. I was so preoccupied I almost missed the turn-off; the realisation that the white car had disappeared then linked to the drifting plume of dust on the side road. I hauled the wheel round and followed.

Praegar's Restaurant was on the edge of a precipice, the parking area carved out of solid rock; the restaurant itself was made of stone with a lot of oak beams and pine timbering, rather like a Swiss chalet and was built right out to overhang the gorge which fell to unknown depths below.

There was distant music of an agreeable, faintly Continental European type and the hum of many voices. The car-park was fairly full so I guessed it was a pretty popular place. I had no trouble slotting in as far from the Rolls as possible and I waited until Stoltz' immaculate figure had disappeared up the flight of rustic stone steps that led to the front of the restaurant.

I got out the Buick, the sun hot on my head,

grateful for the breeze and the perfume of flowers. I wandered over toward the edge of the lot where there was a viewing platform cantilevered out from the cliff-face, bordered by a strong, wooden railing with steel link-mesh to discourage children and potential suicides.

The vertiginous view was certainly spectacular and an old lady with blue-rinsed hair had turned slightly green and was being helped away from the edge by her companion. I stared for a couple of minutes at the razor-edge rock ridges, faintly blurred with lush green vegetation and wild flowers whose riotous colours of yellow and red and gold cloaked the harshness of the terrain. I wondered how long it would take for a body to reach the canyon floor after bouncing off the first rock ridge below.

A crazy idea flickered into my mind then. Supposing Stoltz had something else planned for Kettle. And if he was maybe reconnoitring the terrain before going into action. It sounded ridiculous on the surface; but then so were many of the things Kettle and Elizabeth Goddard had already told me.

I turned away from the observation platform, filing the notion for future reference. I went up the steps to Praegar's Restaurant hoping not only for a good meal but a break that would start making some sense of the set-up.

2

I went to the rustic bar first, done up like a Tyrolean chalet, where even the waiters wore leather shorts and frilled shirts with cross-braces. It was all right if you liked that sort of thing. I could take it or leave it and the cool air circulated by the fans and the even colder lager compensated me for feeling like a fugitive from White Horse Inn.

I spent a quarter of an hour finishing the beer and a second and discreetly pumping the barman about Praegar's and its clientele. That didn't tell me anything I couldn't have found out by using my eyes and as I'd been able to book a table before I came in, the head waitress or whatever she called herself, a tall ash-blonde with a sensational figure, discreetly beckoned from the restaurant entrance and brought the conversation to an end.

The tall number, who had the legend Irene emblazoned in red silk across her right breast, led the way down the big stone-flagged room which was an octagonal shape, built to take advantage of the site, the sharp angles giving sensational overhanging views of the gulf beneath, the mountains in back and the Pacific beyond. Depending on which way one was sitting, of course.

She'd given me a table for two fairly near a

door giving on to a balcony with one of the better views and I took advantage of the breeze and the scenery in front of me. I was talking about Irene now. I preferred her aspect to the scenery outside. I stared with enthusiasm at the name-plate on her right breast. It was a particularly good one though it had heavy competition from its partner on the left.

The girl was maybe aware of this because her eyes flashed and little pink patches started spreading on her cheeks. Not that she looked put out. I guessed she'd seen it all before. So had I come to that but I felt I was getting the better of the trade for the moment. I ordered the blue-plate special and she was gone with a flash of white teeth in the tanned face.

I watched her all the way back across the restaurant floor, thinking this might be one of the better mornings. There was a smattering of applause now and the orchestra leader, a short, plump man with a perspiring face bowed perfunctorily. The band was on a stone plinth in an alcove up the far end and I guessed that, being employees, they weren't entitled to the breeze like the customers.

The orchestra was making with the Gavotte from King Kong and I turned my attention back to the customers scattered around the interior. There were a few privileged tables set out in the open air, on the balconies, beneath the heliotrope umbrellas, but my man wasn't there.

It took me some while to spot him and that was because, paradoxically, he was sitting quite close to me; he was only about two tables away but because of the tropical greenery set about the floor; the jutting angle of one of the pine booths; and the fact that he had his back to me, I hadn't picked him up straight away.

He was sipping a cocktail and obviously waiting for someone because one of the waitresses in frilly Tyrolean costume had come up to him twice already and he'd shaken his head. I wondered if it would turn out to be Pacelli. And if so, why they would choose to meet here where they could only be conspicuous. But I felt my pulse racing a little faster as I finished off my second lager and waited for my blue-plate special to arrive.

The bulk of the Smith-Wesson suddenly seemed to weigh heavily against my muscles through my thin shirt and I shifted to ease the pressure. My own waitress, a slim, undulating brunette was back now, bringing a plate of sea-food and some green salad for starters. I worked my way through that while I kept a discreet eye on Stoltz.

He was reading a newspaper he'd brought in with him. The noise in here was really deafening now and the orchestra was having a job to compete with the customers. I kept my eyes peeled but I couldn't see anyone I knew; certainly not at any of the tables closest to us

114

and certainly not Pacelli.

The girl came when I was least expecting her. I had already started on the main course and was pouring myself a second glass of white wine when I became aware that Stoltz had risen. For a split second I thought he was leaving and then I saw the girl had just arrived at his table. She was taller than I remembered and closer up, the face had all the magic that some half dozen Hollywood movies had engraved on collective folk-memories.

Pepper Coburn wore a wine-red open-neck silk shirt and white linen trousers that revealed her perfect figure and I saw a number of heads turning as she flung the jet-black hair back from her smooth forehead. She was sitting now and the waitress and the girl called Irene had materialised from somewhere like people always do when persons with real charisma appear.

Pepper Coburn had charisma all right; there was no doubt about that and for a moment or two I couldn't reconcile the fact with Stella's comment that Pepper was one of yesterday's stars. Then I remembered she was over thirty compared to today's teenage nymphets and that Hollywood was a tough town; the industry on the rocks; and producers turning desperately from gimmick to gimmick; searching increasingly for ever younger and fresher faces. Completely incomprehensibly in my book, because anyone in his senses would prefer someone like Pepper Coburn to one of the moon-faced juveniles.

But like I said, it's a tough town; and a crazy one at that. I was beginning to realise my journey was a wasted one. This was at best a lovers' meeting; at its most dubious a business one. Unless I could overhear the conversation, which was obviously impossible, I had nothing to show for my money today; or for Kettle's money, I should say. And while I was on Kettle's expenses I might as well enjoy the sunshine as well as endure the shadow. I ordered another half-bottle of wine to go with the dessert.

All the while I was studying the couple. They were obviously in love; one can always tell and without any over-obvious or ostentatious displays of affection, it showed in their glances, in minute gestures and in the occasional intimate pressure of their hands in their gestures across the table.

The orchestra went on sawing away and the atmosphere got more and more soporific. Nothing had happened at the other table; nothing of any importance to me, at any rate. All they'd done was talk in an open fashion and work through their meal. I had seen no suddenly whispered confidences; no passing of packages; letters; or small parcels which might or might not have contained bundles of greenbacks.

You get to tell in my business, which is

based on seventy per cent hunches, backed by a few selected facts. I didn't know whether to be disappointed or relieved. I'd had enough of stake-outs in the rain; of breaking into enclosed premises; of being shot at and hit on the head. It had been a pretty impressive catalogue of disaster in a very few days but it hadn't gotten me any farther forward in the business on which Kettle had engaged me.

I was on coffee when the couple got up to leave. They made a handsome pair. Several times Stoltz had glanced at his expensive gold wristlet watch as though he had some business appointment. I had tossed a coin to see whether I should follow but I'd already made up my mind. It came down heads. I designated the decision after it had fallen.

I let them go and stayed on at the table. I ordered another coffee and a liqueur to go with it. Like I said, Kettle was picking up the tab. And I didn't want to overdo things this afternoon. I was talking about Stoltz and the girl, of course. If I kept on following them around I would only arouse their suspicions; especially in daylight. I could tail them again any time. What I needed was a new angle and a new line of inquiry. Pretty badly.

It was after three when I left Praegar's and the tab made quite a hole in Kettle's expense-chit. Maybe it was delayed shock from my sapping; or just the effect of the large lunch and the wine but it seemed like a hell of a long way back in to L.A. in the heat and the dust.

CHAPTER THIRTEEN

1

I called in at a drug-store on my way across town and phoned Stella.

'Someone rang for you about an hour ago,' she said after I'd got her up to date on the case. Such as it was. She went on before I could interrupt.

'He said it was important but wouldn't give his name over the phone. He sounded young, though.'

I frowned at the white surface of the booth where some young gentleman from one of our more prestigious universities had drawn some interesting graffiti with a really witty caption. I put my head on one side to take in the drawing a little better. Stella was going on now.

'He asked for your home address, said he might call on you later this afternoon. I hope I did right to give it to him, Mike.'

'Sure,' I said. 'It's probably nothing but it could be important. And if mobsters wanted to find out where I live they'd get it through the book without ringing the office.'

I glanced at my watch. It was already half-past four. There was no point in going all the way back in now; especially if someone wanted to see me at Park West. I told Stella to lock up and go home. I'd see her in the morning. I put the phone down and got outside again. As soon as I left the coolness of the store the sun felt hot and harsh on the back of my neck. I walked half a block and found a small, cool bar with Spanish tiles and a shadowy interior.

I got outside an iced beer which perhaps wasn't such a good idea because although it cooled me at the time it was fighting with the wine all the way home. I felt hot and gassy and drenched with perspiration before I'd got halfway, even though I'd wound all the windows down.

It was around half-five when I hit Park West and I was running into the homeward bound traffic making for the freeways. I got off the main-stem at last and tooled on uphill, where the breeze was slightly cooler. I was still a mile or two from my rented house when I had a sudden hunch. Despite what I'd told Stella I felt there might be something suspicious in a stranger who wouldn't give his name asking for my home address.

And my place wouldn't take more than a nail-file to break in the front door. It had been done before. There was a parade of shops serving a housing development off the slip-road and I signalled and pulled the Buick over amid long feathers of dust. I killed the motor and went across to the phone booth that

119

glittered in the metallic sunshine.

I jammed the door open with my foot and dialled my number. I could hear the faint burr of the ringing tone. I let it ring for a couple of minutes and then replaced the receiver before dialling again. I frowned, closed the door and went back to the Buick. If someone had been waiting for me there he might have picked up the phone. Curiosity is one of those things which is difficult to curb.

A friend in the same line of business had once done a similar thing; a hitman in his apartment had taken the call, which enabled him to alert the police. I hadn't really expected anything, but it pays to take simple precautions.

I drove slowly up toward my house, keeping my eyes peeled, noting the automobiles parked on the quiet street, the bulk of the Smith-Wesson in the nylon holster heavy against my chest muscles. I knew most of the heaps; some belonged to neighbours, a number of whom arrived home early on certain days. There wasn't anything suspicious but as I got almost up to my driveway I saw there was a dark half-truck parked under the shelter of the car-port.

I kept on going at the same steady pace, watching the truck in the rear mirror. At the junction with the next road there was a big turning circle for commercial vehicles and I tooled on round and went back down toward my place, taking out the Smith-Wesson and laying it down on the passenger seat, safety on.

This way I could keep the vehicle in sight all the distance and as it slowly grew closer and I could make out the detail I saw that it had the stencil of Acme Autos on the door panel of the driving cab. My first thought was that Big Fat had found out my address and had come to claim damages for his wrecked Rolls.

Then I saw it had nothing to do with him because a thin man in a dark suit was sitting in the driving seat, his eyes closed like the heat had overcome him. I pulled the Buick up on the cement walk next the truck and killed the motor. The sound had awakened the driver because he looked around him like he didn't know where he was.

His face was drenched with perspiration and it took a little while for him to register my presence. I saw then he was the sandy-haired boy who had given me the information at the garage. I wondered why he didn't get out because it must have been searing hot in the cab.

He stirred himself with an effort.

'Mr Faraday?'

I nodded.

'That's the name. What can I do for you?'

The boy closed his eyes with a sudden shiver and a bead of sweat rolled out from underneath his right eyelid. I followed it down, saw something which made my hand tremble on the rim of the hot driving door.

All the front of the boy's shirt beneath the jacket was torn up, mingled with a sticky black mass which glittered. Someone had fired the slug at very close range because there were scorch marks on the remaining fragments of shirt. How he'd survived I didn't know because it was one of the worst gun-shot wounds I'd ever seen.

The boy's eyes were open now. They showed white.

'I came to warn you, Mr Faraday.'

His head sagged over suddenly and hit the edge of the door. The eyes closed again and a thin dribble of black blood ran out the corner of his mouth to mingle with that on the front of his shirt.

I reached in quickly, being careful where I put my hand, felt for the beat of the heart. There was nothing. The boy had died as casually as he'd come into my orbit at the garage.

2

A muscle quivered in my cheek. I felt bad about it. The boy had tried to warn me about something. If I hadn't questioned him at the garage this would never have happened. And I was in a bad spot myself if the police came into it. I looked up and down the eye-aching length of dusty road where the shadows were getting longer and blacker.

I made up my mind quickly. There was only one thing to do and I had to do it at once. I went around to the other door and pulled the boy over, as gently as possible; it was pointless, really, but I felt I owed him a little respect.

There was a length of canvas tarpaulin in rear and I got it out and covered him as he lay on the passenger side of the long bench-seat; I folded the canvas and put it over the sticky mess on the driving seat so that it wouldn't stain my trousers.

Half a minute later I had unlocked the brake and the truck was rolling backwards down the incline; I hoped none of the neighbours had seen me. They'd think I was even crazier than normal. The humped figure at my side vibrated as the truck bumped down on to the road surface. I turned the wheel, putting the gears in neutral and she rolled forward down the steep slope of the road.

I switched the ignition on and waited until I was a couple of hundred yards away before starting the motor in third. Then I maintained a steady fifty and didn't breathe more easily until I was a couple of miles out of Park West, on one of the hill roads connecting with the main stem.

I was oblivious to the heat now or the grit dancing in the wind that came through the open driving window. My brain was like a fruit-machine, ideas whirling round endlessly but failing to cohere and make sense. I knew this boy wouldn't have been very popular with Perrot after what had happened at the garage; and he obviously had suspicions that he'd given me some information.

But that wouldn't have been enough to make him kill the boy, surely. Not that I knew for sure Perrot had anything to do with it. Or with anything else come to that. But I'd already seen that he had a maniacal temper, even over the mild repartee we'd exchanged in the repair shop. And he would have killed me after the Rolls incident.

The more I thought about that aspect the screwier it all appeared. Because all the boy had done was confirm facts already given me by Kettle and Elizabeth Goddard. That the brakes of Kettle's car had been eaten through with acid put there by his partner. The fat man would have known that, probably; not about Stoltz, necessarily, but Kettle would have had to have given him some story about the acid on the cables.

The garage should have reported the matter to the police; Kettle had most certainly paid the fat man a sweetener not to report it. So the car had been repaired and nothing had been said. But that was hardly enough to make the fat man kill his own employee; particularly as the sandy-haired boy had worked on the cables himself. And like he'd told me, he was well aware of the situation. Possibly Perrot paid him a little over the top to be discreet.

I dismissed that possibility out of hand. I wasn't thinking straight this afternoon. But why had the mechanic come to warn me? About what? It was something he could only have learned at his place of employment. If Perrot had been involved and the boy had known my address the fat man would have come out here himself. I was convinced of that; after what I'd done to his vehicle he would have wanted to settle with me personally.

And how had the boy learned who I was and where I lived? I hadn't told him my name or my business. The more I thought about it the bigger tangle it all became. I hadn't forgotten about Pacelli. Or the man in the light raincoat who'd shot at me up at Stoltz' place. There were an embarrassing number of people who could have taken out the boy.

Someone had obviously followed him to my place. They'd silenced him to prevent him from telling me something. They could equally have taken me out too. They hadn't done that. Perhaps because they merely wished to embarrass me with the police by having a corpse on my doorstep.

I had turned the half-truck on to the main-stem now. The bodywork shuddered as I put my toe down, making sure I got through the tail-end of the traffic before the lights at the intersection changed from red to green. I didn't want to be caught at the signals with people in the next lane staring in. Perspiration was cascading down my face and it wasn't entirely caused by the heat.

A fly buzzed suddenly somewhere and then settled on the canvas-shrouded form at my side; it was a funereal image and I made a flailing gesture in the air, rather more angrily than I intended. There was yet another angle I hadn't figured. The boy was wearing quite a smart suit and his hands had been clean and well-scrubbed; so he was off duty when he'd come to see me in his employer's half-truck.

He may have learned something away from his place of work and been shot somewhere else. Miraculously, he had kept going; had escaped his attacker and driven to warn me. I owed him a lot and I felt a heel driving him back into the city to dump him somewhere like a sack of potatoes. I knew the feeling was irrational; that he couldn't know and wouldn't care. But there it was.

I have no conscience about hoods but humanity keeps breaking through where other people are concerned. Perhaps you're becoming human in your old age, Mike, I told myself. I hadn't thought things out very well this afternoon. I was working purely on reflexes now.

I steadied up on the accelerator, dropped back to fifty in the slow inside lane. I hadn't noticed the blue snout of the police car which had been growing in the rear-mirror. It drew level, the grey-haired sergeant at the wheel looking at me incuriously with muddy grey eyes. I gave him a somewhat sickly grin. He didn't seem to see anything wrong though I thought his eyes flickered down to the canvas-covered shape at my side.

But that could have been my overheated imagination. He was cruising steadily at the same speed as I was; I could see a typed list on a sheet of paper taped to his dashboard and the square-jawed young cop in the car with him was reading something out to him in a voice that sounded like powdered granite. The simile wasn't maybe a very good one but it was all my overworked brain was giving me at the moment.

He nodded frostily like he was acknowledging my smile and went on looking at the half-truck. A big man in a Chevy behind him went to lean on his horn-button, saw it was a police car, changed his mind and accelerated unobtrusively over into the third lane. I wondered for a moment whether someone had fingered me by circulating the Acme truck as being stolen. I would never get out if they stopped me.

My stomach sagged toward the floor-boards then. I hadn't looked for the murder weapon. Maybe the pistol was in the truck cabin somewhere. It would have been wiped clean of prints true, but that would mean I couldn't disprove a murder rap. I gave the sergeant my brightest smile, at the same time decelerating, until the snout of the prowl car had drawn ahead.

That was a mistake because he braked sharply and came back level with the cab almost at once. He had seen something wrong, that was for sure. He opened his mouth to say something over the rumble of the motors. We had been running together for only about a minute or so but it seemed like a couple of hours. Before he could get anything out there was a sudden crackle from his radio and a voice started spitting out tinny instructions.

His eyes flickered from me to his companion. His lips opened in an insincere smile.

'You were hitting the gas back there, buddy. Just watch it.'

I nodded, not trusting myself to speak. The young cop flipped a switch and the siren split the air with a deafening wail. The tyres bit and the big prowl car screeched off until it was only a faint blur in the distance. The wheel was so slippery with my perspiration I had to dry it off with my bunched handkerchief before I could handle the steering properly.

It was dusk before I found the right place, beneath some trees in rear of a park. I had chosen the spot carefully because I didn't want to be too far off. I got out the cab quickly, feeling like I was in a spotlight. I put the

Smith-Wesson back in my holster. I took care to dust down the wheel and all the instruments before I quit the cab. I didn't think I'd overlooked anything.

And if I had left any prints I hoped to have the case broken before they could be traced to me. Some possibility, I told myself, looking at my crooked grin in the rear mirror. I waited until a young couple had gone by in the dusk of the neons and then got out the half-truck, locking both doors and putting the keys down the nearest storm-drain.

I looked at my watch. It was still only eight o'clock. I seemed to have aged ten years. I walked a couple of blocks before turning into a hotel bar where I had a stiff bourbon to quiet my nerves. There was no-one much in there and in another ten minutes my toes had stopped doing Fred Astaire routines inside my shoes.

I got in a booth when I finished my drink and dialled Stella's number. She came on straight away. I gave her a discreet report and she told me to stay where I was. She would give me dinner and drive me home afterward.

I thanked her and got out the booth, feeling a little frayed around the edges. I ordered another drink. My nerves were back to normal by the time Stella showed.

CHAPTER FOURTEEN

1

Harry Kettle lived in a penthouse suite over at the Innes Court Apartments. He had another place out at Malibu but I knew that was his main address because Stella had checked. It was dark now and cooler and I drove across town with the windows wound down. I'd bought Stella an early dinner after we'd met up and we'd chewed the situation over.

We hadn't come to any startling conclusions. Her ideas were roughly the same as mine. She hadn't said much but she'd been concerned when I'd filled her in on the garage man's kill. She hadn't approved of my gut-reaction, of course; her natural instinct was that I should have called in the police. That wasn't my style. While I'd been getting myself untangled whatever was rotten about this case would have been spreading unchecked.

Not that it wasn't doing so now, probably; except that I didn't know enough about it to separate the rottenness from the good parts. Such as they were. I stopped beating my brains out and slid the Buick smoothly across into the slow lane. I wasn't in the mood for fast driving tonight and I had too many impressions chasing around inside my skull to make for clear decisions at speed.

It was time I had another chat with Kettle. He'd maybe have some ideas about the situation. I believed him now, of course. And if he was in danger I ought to be doing more to earn my fee. You'll be qualifying for your advanced scout badge soon, Mike, I told myself.

I tooled the Buick into the tiled concourse set next to the Innes Court Apartments and admired a set of three ornamental fountains where naked marble nymphs were frolicking in among the falling fronds of foaming water. It was cool and good in here and smelt of money; from the bougainvillaea and tropical plants outside; to the polished granite façade of the skyscraper; and the heavy bronze front doors.

I gave my name to a uniformed man who sat in a small glass cubicle next the entrance doors and who was pretending to be a commissionaire; but whose square jaw, frosty eyes and heavy bulge under the armpit told me he was an armed guard. He spoke into a small red telephone on the desk in front of him and waited, his eyes fixed up somewhere beyond my shoulder, his well-manicured fingers drumming nervelessly on his blotter.

The phone probably connected with a speaker-system several hundred feet above and he waited quite a few seconds before there was any response. His voice was as soft and bland as a Chinese diplomat's.

'Mr Faraday to see you, Mr Kettle.'

His expression didn't change as the tinny voice went on in the receiver.

'Very well, sir.'

He put the phone down and turned to me, suddenly brisk.

'Mr Kettle says to go on up, sir. Number One Elevator at the other side of the concourse.'

He looked at me absently, obviously assured of my bona-fides.

'I have to stay here, or I'd take you up.'

'It's all right,' I said.

'Penthouse Number 4, sir.'

I nodded and went on over, my number nines slapping echoes off the waxed and polished marble. It seemed far too nice for Harry Kettle. It was unfortunate that his persona didn't match up with his public image. But that's often the way it goes. I got in the panelled elevator which held a bunch of wilting flowers in a silver vase screwed to the wall. I was impressed even before I'd gotten halfway up to the penthouse floor atop the chrome and granite block.

There were only four penthouses, spreading out from a star-shaped concourse. Harry Kettle himself answered my ring. He was dressed in a pale peacock blue dressing gown and he threw it over the back of a leather divan in the hallway. Underneath he wore tan trousers, a wine-coloured open-neck shirt with short sleeves, with a blue silk scarf knotted into the vee.

His face looked greasy and even more unattractive and he had a lot of freckles on his arms. His reddish hair seemed even more phoney than before.

'You must be psychic, Mr Faraday,' he said, closing the door behind me and securing it with a couple of patent locks. 'I've been trying to get hold of you for the past hour.'

'I have some news for you too,' I said.

He shot me a quick glance. There was alarm flickering somewhere in back of his eyes.

'That makes two reasons for meeting, Mr Faraday. Let's go out on the terrace. It's cooler there.'

I followed him across the vast living room with its marble floor, natural stone fireplace wall and sunken dining area, taking in only a vague impression of the expensive-looking oils scattered about against the pale pastel of the other three walls. It was a fine clear night now and the stars were trying to compete with the rivers of green, red and yellow fire that flowed along the canyons of streets below us.

It was a great view from the terrace, but I hadn't come there for that. There were cane tables and chairs set about; a lot of vegetation in trunking and on elegant hardwood frames that screened the place from other similar terraces round about; and brass lanterns burning in overhead fittings that threw down a bland, even light over the tesselated pink paving underfoot.

There was a drinks trolley set alongside an ornamental pool in which carp swam beneath a canopy of vines that would have given shade on the hottest day and Kettle bustled on over, his sneakers making no noise on the tiles.

'Scotch with ice all right?'

'Fine,' I said.

I went and sat down in one of the upright chairs at a big circular cane table fairly near the pool and enjoyed the breeze and the view in equal proportion. Kettle finished fooling around with glasses and a swizzle-stick and came on back. He handed me the crystal goblet and went to sit across from me, his eyes studying my face.

'Will you start or shall I?'

I put my goblet down on the glass top of the table and looked at my fingernails.

'Mine's bad news,' I said. 'Perhaps we'd better start with yours.'

Kettle looked startled but he had a grip on himself tonight. He gave me one of his wry looks.

'I've been having a hard time convincing you about my problems, Mr Faraday. I know it must seem like a lot of hearsay to you. But Miss Goddard also tells me you're a hard man to convince.'

I grinned.

'I'm being converted gradually, Mr Kettle.

What's on your mind?'

Kettle took another heavy pull at his drink.

'You remember the last time we met I was trying to tell you that Stoltz was about to put the clincher on me. He's invited me out to lunch tomorrow.'

'That sounds fairly innocuous,' I said cautiously.

Kettle made an impatient little movement with his head.

'I'd like you to be there, Mr Faraday. You'll need a gun. Herman's got a confidential deal he wants to discuss with me. I'm to go there alone. And it's an ideal place for what I think he has in mind.'

He leaned forward at the table, his knuckles showing white round his glass.

'It's a restaurant up in the mountains, with a sheer drop to the gorge below. A place called Praeger's.'

2

There was a silence so long and so deep that all the noises of the city, including the muffled roar of the traffic that came up to us, seemed completely erased. Kettle had noticed my expression because he said sharply, 'Does that mean anything to you, Mr Faraday?'

'I was there for lunch today, Mr Kettle,' I said. 'Watching your partner without being seen. He was having a very interesting conversation with Pepper Coburn.'

Kettle licked his lips, his eyes glued to my face.

'You been earning your money, Mr Faraday.'

I nodded.

'And that's not all. I've been shot at, roughed up and framed, all within the last forty-eight hours.'

Kettle drew his breath in with a heavy sucking sound but his expression had subtly changed.

'So you do believe me, Mr Faraday? You know what I'm up against.'

'I'm beginning to get the point,' I said. 'I have a little to go on now.'

Kettle nodded, his thoughts evidently far away.

'So they were both there. He and the girl. Setting up things for the knock-over.'

'We don't know that,' I said sharply.

'What do we know, Mr Faraday?'

'Quite a few things,' I said. 'But I'd like to hear your story first. Like you said, there could be some nasty accidents at Praegar's. I was having a few thoughts about that myself.'

'You want me to go?'

I studied his face for a few seconds. He was a frightened man all right.

'Sure,' I said. 'But I won't be far away.'

He gave me a twisted grin.

'I won't go otherwise.'

Kettle thought hard for a moment. He reached for his jacket on the chair next him and drew out a chequebook.

'Bounced, fired at and framed, eh? Seems like you're worth more than I thought.'

'I won't argue with that,' I said. 'But forget the money for the moment. We'll sort that out at the end of the case.'

He gave another grimace.

'Assuming I'm still around.'

'You'll be around,' I said. 'Just so long as you follow my instructions.'

He looked at me with a glimmer of respect.

'Rough stuff is your business, Mr Faraday. He wants me to meet him at one o'clock.'

'Go there,' I said. 'I'll be ahead of you at twelve. You got a table booked?'

'He's already fixed it,' Kettle said. 'Number 24.'

'That's something,' I said. 'I'll try and get one close by. I'll ring Praegar's later.'

Kettle leaned forward at the table. His face looked suddenly haggard again. He was really his age without the makeup and special lighting.

'What's this all about, Mr Faraday?'

'I'll get to it,' I said. 'I want to hear your end first.'

He gulped.

'Stoltz came up to my office this afternoon. We went over a few routine things. Then he mentioned this big housing development he's had brewing for the last year or two. Apparently it's reached a crucial point. He suggested meeting at Praegar's. Then, after lunch we're to go see the architect on site. It's quite near to Praegar's.'

'So if anything doesn't happen at lunch there might be a lot of opportunities among the cranes and the heavy equipment,' I said.

Kettle nodded, his face white.

'That's about it, Mr Faraday. That's what I figure, anyway.'

I stared at him in silence for a moment or two longer.

'What's the name of this place? I ought to know just in case.'

Kettle still looked frightened.

'Just in case what?'

I shrugged.

'We've got to think of every eventuality. I'll have to tail you when you leave. Supposing I got blocked in a traffic jam. If I didn't know where you were heading I wouldn't be able to show up.'

Kettle gulped. His face was resuming its normal colour.

'Sure, Mr Faraday. I didn't understand. I thought you meant something else.'

I shook my head.

'Don't look on the dark side. That's what I'm trying to avoid. What's the name of the place?'

Kettle had his eyes fixed up over my head somewhere, like he hadn't heard the question.

'You're carrying a gun, Mr Faraday?' he asked anxiously.

'Sure as hell I am,' I said. 'Especially after what happened.'

'What did happen?'

I shook my head impatiently.

'Afterward. We're taking your story first. And I'm still waiting for my answer.'

Kettle pulled himself together. He'd got one of the worst cases of jitters I'd ever seen.

'The development,' he said tonelessly. 'It's called Sunset Homes. Not very original, I'm afraid. But it directly faces the setting sun, you see. It's about two miles up the canyon from Praegar's.'

I made a note on my pad.

'What makes you think this is anything different from a normal business conference?'

Kettle gave me one of his bitter smiles. He was pretty good at them and they had a startling effect on anyone used only to his TV image.

'What normal business conference, Mr Faraday? Almost every time I've met Stoltz for some specific purpose the last few months it's had a potentially lethal outcome so far as I'm concerned.'

I inclined my head.

'You have a point there.'

He grunted.

139

'You're getting the idea, Mr Faraday. I just have a gut instinct that tomorrow's meeting will be the clincher. My partner has something special organised. So I'd like you to be close by.'

'I'll be on the table, disguised as a salt cellar,' I promised him.

Kettle grunted again. The red spots were back on his cheek-bones, making him look like the little pierrot figure.

'Your sense of humour is one of the hardest things to bear,' he said sadly.

'It's just reaction,' I said. 'I've been exposed to yours for years.'

He did actually smile at that, clicking his tongue like some old fashioned maiden aunt.

'Touché, Mr Faraday.'

'I didn't know you spoke German,' I told him.

I ignored his pained expression. It hadn't been very funny but we were pretty short on laughs on this case so far and I was only trying to lighten the atmosphere.

'That all you have to tell me?' I said.

He nodded frostily, resuming his old manner.

'For the moment.'

I ignored that. I had other fish to fry.

'Time you showed your hand, Mr Faraday.'

'Four aces,' I said. 'Murder; attempted murder; attempted assault; and assault with a deadly weapon. Chew on those for starters.'

CHAPTER FIFTEEN

1

Kettle didn't actually turn white this time but he went a mottled mauve colour. He had difficulty getting his words out. When he did his voice was a strangled croak.

'I hope you're joking, Mr Faraday.'

'I can take a joke with the best of them,' I said. 'But these jokers were serious.'

Kettle's eyes were like two tiny pinholes in his face.

'You want to tell me about it?'

'Some of it,' I said.

He tried to get a grip on his nerves, didn't make too good a job of it.

'Why only some of it?'

'Because you're frightened enough already, Mr Kettle. I don't want you going to pieces tomorrow.'

Kettle stared bleakly at the glass table top. It didn't seem to give him any comfort.

'You're honest, at any rate.'

'I thought that's why you hired me,' I said.

I had my eyes on Kettle's trembling fingers. He took his hand off the table and put it down at his side. Then he seemed to remember his drink and picked it up, draining the remainder of the contents at a gulp.

'That won't help very much,' I said.

Kettle shrugged. He got up, sweat glistening in among the roots of his dyed red hair.

'But it will help,' he said.

He went across the roof garden to mix himself another, leaving me to look at the tropical vegetation, the fish in the pool, the evening breeze stirring the tassels on the ornamental umbrella, and the distant lights of L.A. I took a short sip at my own drink and then Kettle was back, his anxious eyes on my face.

'I'm waiting, Mr Faraday,' he said, trying to keep his voice steady.

'I was up at Stoltz' place,' I said. 'He didn't see me. But someone else did. Tall character in a light raincoat and a fedora. He took a shot at me while I was outside the house keeping tabs on your partner and his girlfriend.'

Kettle made a faint choking noise down in his throat.

'Herman didn't know you were there?'

I shook my head.

'My guess is this character had him under observation too. Maybe it was his way of warning off competition.'

Kettle knotted up his brows like he had some insuperable problem. He looked like I felt, come to think of it.

'You mentioned murder, Mr Faraday.'

'We'd best leave that for the moment,' I said. 'I want you steady enough to go through

142

your part tomorrow. Someone tried to frame me by dumping a corpse on my doorstep. I had to transport it to the other side of the city.'

This was a slight exaggeration but it had the proper effect on Kettle; he gave another choking noise and his eyes were glazed this time.

I went on before he could finish the Academy Award stuff.

'You probably wouldn't have known the victim, except in the most casual way. None of this makes any sense to me. I'm hoping you might come up with some ideas.'

'Give me some hard facts and I'll do my best, Mr Faraday,' Kettle said with a flash of his old spirit.

He swilled his drink round in the bottom of his glass and waited for me to continue.

'There's two people or maybe two factions involved in this,' I said. 'Stoltz is employing a professional hitman called Pacelli. I followed him from Stoltz' office. He went to a fruit trucking concern on the other side of town. That's when the lights went out. Either he sapped me or someone else on his behalf.'

Kettle licked his lips and took another swig from his glass.

'Like I said you're sure earning your money, Mr Faraday,' he mumbled.

'Pacelli mean anything to you?' I said.

Kettle shook his head. He shivered like the warmth of the night breeze had suddenly turned glacial.

'No. I don't move in that world. But if Pacelli is a professional hitman, you better be good if I'm going to stick my neck out tomorrow.'

'I am good, Mr Kettle,' I said softly. 'But I'm not asking you to do anything out of the ordinary. If I hadn't told you this you'd have gone out to Praegar's tomorrow anyway. And you won't be running any more risk than you have been these past weeks.'

Kettle ran a greasy finger along his nose.

'You think Pacelli fixed those brakes, brought that hillside down?'

'Could be,' I said. 'But it's immaterial, really. If Stoltz is out to get you he'd hardly do all these things in person. It would be too risky.'

'So Pacelli could have closed that freezer door?' Kettle said thoughtfully.

His voice was so low I had a job to make out the sense of his words.

'But we have a firm link between Pacelli and Stoltz,' I said. 'Later on I went back to the office in rear of the fruit warehouses. I found correspondence and a bundle of bills which tied the two in.'

Kettle's eyes were burning. He nodded his head a few times like I'd said something profound.

'That's it, then, Mr Faraday. Like I said, you've done well. Don't think I'm not grateful.'

'Skip it,' I said. 'The case is nowhere near over yet.'

The expression in Kettle's eyes had changed again.

'You said something about attempted assault . . .' he began.

I shook my head.

'We'll leave that for the moment. It's got something to do with the kill on my doorstep. I haven't been able to work it out yet. But it will surface in due time.'

Kettle took another cautious sip at his drink like it might bite him.

'You've given me a lot to think about, Mr Faraday.'

'I'm glad about that, Mr Kettle,' I said. 'It will be good to share the burden.'

He gave me a sour look but he didn't rise to it.

'You want me to ring you in the morning?'

'Not unless anything else happens,' I said. 'Otherwise, go ahead with Stoltz. Like I said I'll be out at Praegar's in good time.'

I lit a cigarette and held out my glass for a re-fill. I was getting hoarse with all this talking. Kettle took the hint. I waited until he'd come back with the drink and re-seated himself. I toasted him silently over the rim of my glass.

'I'm still waiting for your ideas,' I said.

Kettle scratched around among the dyed roots of his unnatural-looking hair.

'I never heard of Pacelli, Mr Faraday. If

someone other than you was watching Stoltz' place your ideas are as good as mine. Sorry to be so unhelpful but all this is your department. That's why I called you in.'

I grinned.

'You're right, Mr Kettle. Just play your part tomorrow and we may learn something further.'

A large carp came up to the surface of the pool to gulp air and stared at me briefly. He looked as blank as my thoughts on the case.

I looked out at the garish dusk where a thousand neon signs made a sort of hideous daylight bisected by the darker canyons of boulevards; a never-ending stream of yellow fire from headlamps making a sluggish lava-flow as far as the eye could see. Anonymous as a paper cup Chandler had called it; he was about right.

I finished my drink and got up to go. Kettle lingered helplessly at the table, as though trapped there by a paralysis of the will.

'I'm relying on you,' I said.

He raised his eyes at last, giving a bitter laugh that seemed to echo metallically round the penthouse terrace.

'I could say the same, Mr Faraday.'

I went on out and left him there in limbo between the echoing twilight of the city and the cloaking darkness of the sky.

I was up early next morning and on the road by eight o'clock. Stella just beat me in by a few minutes and I gave her a brief rundown on the situation while the coffee was brewing. She was silent as I finished, the disturbed air of the fan making little ripples in her hair.

It was sunny today and the plastic blinds at the window were making a harsh slatted effect on the floor. Later, when the sun moved around it would be more tolerable. I sat back at my old broad-top, listening to the rat-tat of Stella's heels as she went over to fetch the coffee. My skull was back to normal now so I guessed the slicing-bar merchants had finished their performance.

Until the next time, that is. Stella came and sat in the client's chair opposite, giving me a few letters from the previous night to sign.

'They found the boy,' she said at last. 'There was a paragraph in this morning's Examiner. The proprietor of the garage, Perrot, was all cut up about it.'

'I'll bet,' I said.

I nuzzled into my coffee and took the first sip. Stella sat watching me, all sorts of questions chasing themselves across her face. I kept her waiting for the answers.

'So what was with Kettle?' she said.

'He seems a badly frightened man,' I said.

Stella shrugged.

'We knew that already,' she told the filing cabinet.

I let that go. It was hot this morning and I had the coffee to concentrate on. Today Stella wore a pale blue dress with a sort of ballerina skirt that was buckled in at the waist and set her tanned legs off to advantage. She leaned back in the chair and cupped her hands over one smooth knee like she knew what I was thinking.

'You think he'll turn up at Praegar's?' she said.

I gave her a long look.

'He'd better,' I said. 'Otherwise we've no way of cracking the case.'

Stella smiled faintly.

'I hope your aim is steady, Mike. If anything pops things might be tricky in a crowded restaurant.'

'I hope it won't be in a crowded restaurant,' I said. 'I'm putting my money on the building site.'

Stella's smile widened.

'Kettle's putting his money on you, Mike.'

I leaned back in my chair.

'Meaning what? If things go wrong I'll resign from the case.'

A frown chased itself across Stella's forehead.

'That may not be very satisfactory for

Kettle. If things go wrong he may resign from life.'

I grinned.

'In that event I'll refund his money.'

Stella got up with a little impatient movement and brushed a strand of hair from her eyes.

'Be serious, Mike.'

'I am serious, honey. Kettle's not exactly my favourite character.'

Stella looked at me with very blue eyes.

'But he is your client,' she said softly.

I nodded.

'I won't argue with that,' I said.

CHAPTER SIXTEEN

1

There was a rainbow arcing over the dim blue edges of the hills as I drove out to Praegar's and I ran into thin sheets of rain from time to time. It was a curious situation, driving on a dry highway which looped up in hairpins, the sun shining; and then going into misty drizzle on wet roads which were as soaked as though it had been raining for hours.

It's a freak condition we get from time to time and I could see where dry and wet sections of roadway met with almost mathematical precision. I had plenty of time and so I had no need to hurry. I'd checked the Smith-Wesson and had a spare clip of shells in the nylon holster, just in case. The .38 made a comforting pressure against my shoulder muscles as I tooled the Buick round the curves, the tyres singing and throwing up fine feathers of spray.

I was out into dry air and sunshine again now, and I paused at a junction, making sure I was on the right section. Traffic was thin at the moment and I was content to let the flow overtake me, my thoughts knocking around inside my skull with the effortless triviality of a fruit machine.

It was only just turned ten a.m. and I was earlier than expected. I figured I would hit Praegar's at around eleven and that would give me plenty of time to go over the ground. I didn't think anything would happen at the restaurant but like Stella said one couldn't be too careful. I wanted to see where table 24 was located. Stella had rung the restaurant and managed to get table 28 for me. That should be close enough to make out what was going on and to intervene if necessary; but far enough off to avoid being picked out by Stoltz.

Of course, if Pacelli was working for him he might know about me anyway. Unless someone else had slugged me. The whole thing was a tangle. But it was Pacelli I was worried about. If my figuring was correct he'd be setting the pace; and he was the one I'd got to stop and from whom Kettle had most to fear. I started the wipers again, my thoughts interrupted by the sudden belt of rain which was making an almost impenetrable haze across the roadway ahead.

I peered through the arc of the windshield, conscious of the water drumming off the bonnet and streaming from the roof. It was heavy, vicious stuff and the suddenly gusting wind caused me to slacken speed a little, even though I hadn't been exactly burning up the highway. I was high in the hills now, the rainbow occasionally hidden by foliage or the shoulders of the mountains as the road continued to twist and turn.

There was some dangerous terrain here and once I passed a white metal edging fence where the railings had been smashed clean away; the highway department had put plastic-hooded winking lights on stands here, presumably to warn drivers until the fencing could be repaired. If a truck had gone through the driver wouldn't have stood a chance; it was at least a three hundred foot drop to the jagged surface of the canyon floor below.

Pleasant thoughts, Mike, I told myself. I was coming out the rain belt now and I switched off the wipers, grateful for the warmth of the air and the dryness of the road ahead. By the time I'd gone another half mile steam was rising from the bonnet and the Buick's bodywork was dry.

I'd been so preoccupied today that I'd hardly been conscious of the Pacific beneath the driving sheets of rain and cloud and the outlines of Mount Baldy were hidden somewhere in scads of rain that resembled greyish mist. It was still only around a quarter to eleven when I hit Praegar's and tooled the Buick on into the rock-floored parking-lot that had the sensational view and the cantilevered viewing platforms.

It hadn't been raining here and the sun was shining like there was no such thing in the weather charts as moisture. My shirt was sticking limply to my back as I went over toward the area where the most spectacular view was. The car-park was about half-full and I went down the aisles of vehicles casually, reading the names and addresses on the licence details strapped round the steering posts.

If I was looking for Pacelli's heap I was out of luck; he'd probably use an assumed name or a borrowed vehicle. Supposing that all my hunches about Kettle's problems were true. Which was asking a lot under the circumstances. I paused by the balcony and stared down into the gorge. I didn't bother to check out all the cars. That was only asking for trouble. There was certainly no sign of Stoltz' Rolls.

But if they weren't meeting until midday

there was no reason for there to be. I paused by the railing like I was held there for some purpose that was vague even to myself. The balcony itself was levered out from the cliff face; then it fell for perhaps a dozen feet on to great slabs of rock that shaded to the blue-grey distances of the gorge. Growing from crevices in the rock were small trees and bushes that masked the actual cliff face beyond from the spectator's sight. Far below was an S-bend of road with a couple of cars parked in a layby.

But what I could see was enough. If the drop had been sheer it would have been sufficient to give the viewer nosebleed. But looking up toward the great Swiss chalet of the restaurant itself I could see that the balconies there, some of which had tables dotted about, overlooked a drop which fell clear to the valley floor.

That could be important because if anything bad happened up here I wanted to know the lay-out as well as possible. So I stood and smoked a cigarette for a few minutes longer and memorised the details. There was a small red and white flag flying atop the building which made the place look like a corner of some remote Swiss canton on a travel poster.

I snapped out of the euphoric mood and went up the front steps of Praegar's at a fast clip, the Smith-Wesson in its nylon harness jolting against my chest. It was exactly eleven o'clock when I hit the entrance lobby.

153

I checked on the tables first of all, before
going through into the bar for a drink. The tall
number, who was still called Irene, if the
legend emblazoned on her breast was anything
to go by, uncoiled herself from her
conversation with the barman and came on
over, her tread youthful and springy on the
soft carpeting. The look in her eye made me
feel like we were old friends.

'You're early, sir,' she said after I'd
identified myself.

'I finished up my appointment ahead of
schedule,' I said. 'I'd just like to check on the
table and then I'll go through for a drink.'

'Surely.'

I followed her through into the big
octagonal restaurant, admiring her action all
the way.

'I think you'll be comfortable here.'

She indicated a table for two that was
screened on one side by ornamental panelling
in pine that was carved elaborately in what was
evidently meant to be the Swiss style; and on
the restaurant side by a low border of tropical
plants set in trunking at floor level. I glanced
across quickly, saw tables 26 and 27.

I realised by the lay-out that table 24 was
one of those outside on the balcony, screened

from the glare of the sun by one of the striped umbrellas. I hadn't figured on this. It was a table for four but there were only two chairs. Shading my eyes against the glare outside, I saw that I would be able to cover both Stoltz and Kettle if I shifted my chair over a little in the alcove.

It might make matters complicated but it couldn't be helped; and Stoltz wouldn't be able to see me in the dimness of the interior, especially if he sat in the chair sidewise on to me. The distance was only a few yards in any case.

The tall number had misinterpreted my silence.

'Something wrong, sir? We could perhaps change the seating arrangement . . .'

She looked quickly out toward the balcony.

'I guess you'd prefer to sit outside. Most of our customers like the balconies.'

She shrugged.

'But for safety reasons we're compelled to have fewer tables out there than we'd like.'

She made a wry mouth.

'And they usually get booked up weeks ahead.'

'This is fine,' I said. 'All right to have a look out there?'

The tall number smiled.

'Of course.'

She took the ten-spot I gave her and put it in the pocket of her Swiss-style apron. There was a faint flush on her cheek.

'There was really no need . . .'

'Think nothing of it,' I said. 'Comes out of expenses. And this must be a hard racket.'

She smiled.

'It's certainly hard on the feet. But thanks just the same.'

I left her and went out on the big balcony; the air was pleasantly cool under the umbrellas. There were only four tables on this side, with glass doors at intervals leading back into the restaurant. 24 was the one nearest my table.

I leaned over the railing. Like I figured the view to the gorge floor, where the white ribbon of a stream foamed and tumbled among the rocks, was stomach-turning. There was a sheer drop from the balcony. No-one could come in—or get out—from that way.

I came back in to find the head waitress or whoever she was, had gone. The restaurant was empty at this time of day; I'd guessed it maybe would have been popular for morning coffee and things like that but perhaps it was all too much trouble for a place on this scale. They would have to re-lay all the tables for lunch. I stood and admired the stone and pine interior; the massive beams of the roof and the Swiss-style table-cloths before walking back into the bar.

By contrast this was fairly crowded and I kept my eyes peeled but I couldn't see anyone

I knew. When my eyes had adjusted to the light I ordered a cold lager from one of the barmen and took it over to study the big printed menu for the day that was hung in a glass case on the far wall, near the entrance doors.

From here I could keep my eye on the car-park and I'd be sure to see Stoltz' white Rolls. If he was driving it today, of course. He might come early too, in order to prepare some sort of reception for Kettle and in that case I could learn something. Or not. It was that sort of situation. The lager was good and I was enjoying its iced progress down my throat.

The menu looked equally good and I mentally reserved a couple of courses for when I got back inside the restaurant. There were one or two waitresses fussing around inside now, and a plump woman, looking tailor-made for the part in her tight-fitting Swiss outfit switched on a light over the restaurant reception desk.

The thin, high note of a violin sounded as an early-comer on the orchestra stand started tuning his instrument. I glanced at my watch. It was almost half eleven. I had plenty of time still. Through the glass wall outside more automobiles were beginning to arrive; I could hear the faint sound of engines throbbing and see blue coils of exhaust smoke dispersed by the wind.

The bar was beginning to fill up too; I was

in a good position here as I could see everyone in the bar; most of the restaurant through the glass wall; and a good deal of the parking-lot. I made like I was still intensely interested in the bill of fare and studied the clientele over the rim of my glass. I had drawn an entire blank so far. There was no-one around who looked even remotely like a suspect in a B-movie, let alone in real-life.

But that didn't prove anything. I moved over to the bar again, letting the conversation wash over me. I ordered another lager, studied the crowd while I was waiting for it to come. There were some good-looking women up at the far end. Next time I glanced at my watch it was a quarter of twelve. I was looking at a particularly well-built number who seemed to be wearing a silver lamé sweater which was why I missed them coming in.

I pulled my eyes from the restaurant over to the mirror set atop the bar. That was when I saw Kettle and Stoltz standing by the entrance doors.

CHAPTER SEVENTEEN

1

I stood still, my senses alert. My eyes were stabbing every which way now. Kettle and his companion were coming down toward me; they passed and went on to the far end of the bar. Kettle didn't glance at me; he looked miserable enough already and he would have been bound to have given himself away. I wasn't concerned with them for the moment.

I was looking for someone else because any danger in here wouldn't be coming from Stoltz; not unless he was a nutcase; and he was far from that according to my information. The bar was thinning out a little as people drifted into the restaurant in twos and threes; the orchestra had struck up behind the glass wall; the thin, syrupy melody made me feel like an extra in some old thirties musical.

I couldn't see anyone who shouldn't have been around and when I glanced up the far end Stoltz and Kettle were sitting at one of the cane tables set against the wall separating the bar from the restaurant. I walked round into the restaurant, taking it nice and slow. I'd still be able to see them from my table. The little bald man was up on the stone plinth now, waving his stick like he was Toscanini on one of his better days.

He finished as I got to Table 28, and there was a smattering of applause from the few tables that were occupied. The tall number was coming over but I held up my lager glass and said I'd enjoy the breeze and order lunch later.

I had a fine view of Stoltz and Kettle from

here; they seemed the best of friends and were having quite an animated conversation. Kettle appeared to be keeping up his end all right. I looked at Stoltz' clear-minted Patric Knowles profile and then at Kettle's worn, sad clown's face surmounted by the dyed hair. They were certainly an odd couple to be partners in any enterprise. But then I guess one could say that about most marriages, let alone business arrangements.

You're getting cynical in your old age, Mike, I told myself. I leaned back in my chair, ostensibly studying the menu but really ranging over the people drifting in; or already seated at the tables studying their menus or wine-lists. There was no-one and nothing that fitted my bill. Which made me more suspicious than ever. I could see the partners at the bar table out the corner of my eye and after a little they got up and drifted toward the entrance.

I swivelled a little in my chair so I could follow them. They were about a hundred yards off still and I made sure they were coming directly into the restaurant before resuming my previous position. A shadow fell across the table as they passed in front of me, going out to the balcony.

I had my nose buried in the menu by this time and over the top could see that Stoltz had seated himself opposite with Kettle in the facing seat. Today Stoltz wore an elegant grey chalk-stripe suit that looked like something

160

out of an Antonioni movie and he appeared to be in good form, judging by the smiles and laughter to which he was treating his sour-faced partner.

He put on a good act and I admired his technique all through my ordering of lunch; I decided to call it quits at two lagers and settled for some fruit juice. I would need a clear head later, though I guessed Kettle's greatest danger might come up at the building site. I'd play it by ear all the way. I finished the first course and kept my eyes open. The restaurant was pretty full now and what with all the noise of conversation and the clatter of cutlery it was difficult to keep one's concentration.

The woman called Irene was back again. She called a shapely-looking teenager over and transmitted my order. The second girl was back in an astonishingly short time with my selection. I worked my way through the stuff, enjoying it twice as much knowing that Kettle, sitting opposite, was picking up the tab. Today's assignment could have been monotonous; the normality of the restaurant with its air of pleasure; the clatter of cutlery; the clink of glasses; and the murmur of conversation numbed the mind.

That could be fatal also and I snapped out of it quickly. My brain was sharp; I'd had only the two lagers earlier and fruit juice since but the warmth of the air and the general atmosphere of the place was soporific and sapping to the will. I glanced over at Table 24. Stoltz had his shoulders bowed as he studied the menu and a tall waitress with red hair was bent over Kettle's shoulder as he selected something from the wine list.

His eyes were glazed and he looked pretty strained to me; but then he would be in his situation. For a moment or two his glance caught mine and had then passed on in an attempt at casualness. I was glad I hadn't been sitting any nearer. If I had, Kettle's general demeanour would have signalled the shots to Stoltz in a few seconds.

I glanced at my watch. It was already almost one o'clock and the place was even fuller than before. There was hardly a table unoccupied and it was getting more difficult to keep tabs on people passing to and fro. I was on the dessert now; a sort of ice-cream gateau which had been made with old cognac and thin layers of biscuit which left a sharp aftertaste in the mouth.

Coffee was on the table before anything else happened. Both men at Table 24 had their heads bowed over the cloth, looking at something on the table between them. I couldn't see what it was but I figured it was probably plans, a blueprint or perhaps correspondence concerned with the building project they were going to see after lunch.

It was very sunny now and there was a slight dazzle behind the two men, coming from the strong light flooding the edge of the balcony. I shaded my eyes with the menu and kept a sharp look-out still. There were several people quitting the balcony, evidently from tables farther down. I noticed an elderly couple behind Kettle and the red-haired waitress, who were bunched together in the narrow aisle.

There were also two people waiting at the balcony entrance, partly blocking the view. They were evidently going to one of the balcony tables. They were a young couple and I didn't give them further thought. For a few seconds I lost sight of Stoltz and Kettle at Table 24. When they were in view again there was a drastic change.

It had started with a slight murmur from the diners farther down. There was a sort of eddy in the people coming to and from the balcony and as it cleared I could briefly see Kettle. There was a big man coming out; probably from one of the far balcony tables. Or he may have gone in from the main restaurant and walked along the balcony. I hadn't figured on that. But then it must have been one of my off days.

There was something vaguely familiar about him but I couldn't make it out at first because of the sun-dazzle. That had probably been carefully calculated as well. He floated in and out of focus and I knew there was something badly wrong. He had a long brown paper parcel under his arm and he started tearing the paper off as he came on down toward the people bunched at the balcony entrance.

He went on past the table occupied by Kettle and Stoltz and I lost him for a few seconds; the strange murmuring continued and there was a curious eddying motion among the people clustered at the entrance. I was already rising from the table when the red-headed waitress hit the deck.

The hard-minted face of Angelo Pacelli suddenly swam into focus as he whirled, throwing the brown paper wrapping to the floor. The twin barrels of the big shotgun were levelled at Harry Kettle's head.

2

I swore. Screams were erupting round me now as I lunged forward, reaching for the Smith-Wesson. Praegar's was a seething mass of people, wavering to and fro like an uncontrollable crowd at a baseball game. I collided with an old lady before I'd gone a yard from my table and she went down with an agitated squawk. I went down with her. I forgot about the Smith-Wesson. There were far too many people in here.

The crowd parted as the people on the balcony dived out the way. I saw Kettle then, his face grey with fear; he had hold of the shotgun barrels and was holding them

164

desperately away from him. I couldn't see Pacelli because of the milling crowd. I guessed he'd had some trouble because of the closeness of the people. If he'd wanted to take Kettle out he had to work in the confines of the balcony and now there were too many diners there.

Probably somebody had passed in front of the barrels at the critical moment. He was a pro and he wouldn't have fired unless he was certain of taking out his target. I was cursing myself for professional incompetence. I had half-decided in my mind that if the hit came it would be at the building site. Maybe Stoltz wanted me to think that way. And he would be in the clear if Kettle was hit.

Two more seconds only had passed and I was on my feet again, ignoring the old lady's shrieks. Still no explosion had come so it was too late. I caught another glimpse of Kettle, hanging grimly on to the barrels; they were swivelled now, facing down toward the table. Stoltz had risen, his back to me.

When the blast of both barrels came it was like Hiroshima; the double explosion slapped back from the restaurant walls in a thunder-clap detonation among the confusion of cries and shuffling feet. The orchestra's waltz had ground to a halt some while before. I was still a little way from the table and I couldn't see what had happened. I had the Smith-Wesson out now, leaving the safety on. I wouldn't use it unless it was absolutely necessary but it made me feel better.

Half the people at Praegar's seemed to be lying on the floor, while the others were in flight. There was a big blockage of people at the balcony entrance and I had to use my elbows to get through. There was no sign of Pacelli by now; but then there never is when one's dealing with a pro. Kettle was lying half-in, half-out the wreckage of the table, which had overturned. There was a lot of blood about.

His face was as grey as the rearside of an elephant. The big shot-gun was lying at the edge of the balcony, both shells fired. Kettle moved then. His eyes were dilated with pain and horror. His fingers trembled as he grasped my arm.

'My God, Faraday, that was close!'

His eyes were clearing now as he levered himself up.

'You took your time.'

I'd forgotten about Stoltz. He was lying half covered by the once-white tablecloth which had been scorched and torn by the blast as Kettle had wrenched the barrels round. I didn't bother to look any further. The big shells would have taken his head off at that range.

Kettle was getting up.

'Jeeze, what a mess.'

My ears were still singing with the

166

concussion. People were getting up too. They looked dazed.

'Stay here,' I told Kettle. 'Nothing else will be happening now.'

I got another cloth from a pile standing on a side-table in the corner and put it over what was left of Kettle's partner. Then I went down the restaurant at a run, throwing off the Smith-Wesson safety, searching the sun-baked vista of the parking-lot through the glass wall.

I could hear a car motor. There was something wrong; either the carburettor was flooded or it was missing somehow. I got outside and pounded over toward the Buick, the breath hissing in my throat.

But the adrenalin was working at last and I was functioning as normal; the atmosphere had been claustrophobic in Praegar's and I'd been considerably shaken. But at least my client had come out in one piece, thanks to his own initiative. I'd sort out the rest later. I could see the bulky form of Pacelli now. He wore a grey light-weight suit and he was seated in the driving seat of a big black Caddy up in the far aisle of the parking-lot.

A fat man with a smear of white mustache was just driving a scarlet sport-job in. He looked a slob but he was pretty quick on the uptake when I explained what I wanted. He put the car broadside on, blocking the exit aisle. I'd told him to keep his head down and a few seconds later I saw him lighting out for the

167

restaurant, crouching on all fours.

I was already running down the next line of parked automobiles, keeping a tight watch on Pacelli. He'd seen the fat man's manoeuvre and now he must have spotted my head over the top of the parked vehicles because a slug spanged viciously off metal somewhere.

I got down, crawling in rear of the cars. Pacelli had given up. He couldn't get out the way he'd come in and if he took time to reverse he would have to come down the next aisle past me; assuming he could start the motor.

I kept my head close to the ground. I could see his feet going away fast. I got up and started to follow, tucking my elbows into my sides, my heart pumping in my throat. Pacelli had no time for me; he was going really fast, making for the railed-in enclosure with the spectacular view.

I was so taken with this fantastic sight that I almost forgot to follow. It was one of the most incredible things I'd ever seen. The big man with an athlete's stride didn't even hesitate. He jumped atop the broad wooden balustrade and then launched himself into space. I was almost up to the rail now and I could see what he was after.

I guessed he'd thought it all out long before. It was his planned escape route. The rocks below must have been some fifteen feet down and sloped, like I said. He landed awkwardly and skidded; then he had twisted aside and gone into the shelter of the thick shrubbery which grew from the cracks in the rock. Far below the sun glittered on metal. There was only one automobile parked in the dusty layby. I guessed Pacelli would have a back-up. It would be my last chance if I couldn't nail him now.

My own actions surprised even me. I put the Smith-Wesson back in my holster. Then I went back a ways and sprinted down. I must have looked an even madder sight than the hitman. I jumped on to the bonnet of the nearest parked car and did a sky-dive clear over the top of the railing in the direction Pacelli had taken.

The rocks came up toward me, looking as unlikely and dangerous as the deck of an aircraft carrier to a pilot landing in a Pacific gale.

CHAPTER EIGHTEEN

1

I was so mad at Pacelli I don't think I would have done it in cold blood. I had no time for fear. The rock was coming up disastrously fast and I tried to twist my body round in mid-air. There wasn't a chance really, but somehow I landed without breaking anything, skidding an agonising distance along the steeply sloping shelf toward the big drop before I braked with my heels.

Every muscle in my body ached and I could see blood pouring down my left hand where I'd grazed it on landing. I ran, crab-wise down the grey, wrinkled slab that beat the sun back like heavy hammer strokes, conscious of white faces starting to line the balustrade. One wingless Icarus this afternoon was incredible; two was too much.

I could hear a thrashing in the bushes ahead, was conscious of the pain of my body and the wind whipping at my face. Sweat ran down into my eyes and particles of dust and grit from the surface of the rocks was stinging my pupils. I got into the shelter of the nearest clump of bushes and took stock.

There were faint noises coming over the gusting wind; they were cautious, scraping sounds like I was making myself. The sort of noises a man makes who's been to his physical limit and in whom reaction is now setting in. Like me. I was beginning to tremble violently and having trouble co-ordinating my movements. I grinned bleakly and shuffled toward the distant sounds, keeping a thick screen of bushes between myself and the source of the noise.

The view from here was even more spectacular than from the parking lot, partly because of the lack of security that the railing had given but I had no time for the Thomas Cook stuff. I moved over cautiously, trying to control the reaction, being careful where I put my hands and feet. I had one advantage over Pacelli; he probably didn't figure I'd followed.

That would call for a madman of his own class and there wouldn't be many of those about at the best of times. I was coming to the end of the screen. We were on a shelf of rock like a great upturned soup plate and it teetered up to a knife-edge in front; it was all striated and split with earth convulsions in past ages and at first I couldn't see any sign of Pacelli.

Then I heard movement and creeping forward was able to see down into a sort of chimney where the two halves of rock had split away. The granite was all ragged and studded with razor sharp edges and I guessed even Pacelli wouldn't be crazy enough to risk that. I moved on over, finding a place narrow enough to jump across, conscious of the vast blue space that fell to the floor of the gorge at my right.

There were big boulders up ahead, like giant billiard balls tossed around by some cosmic eruption and I got one between me and the exposed face of the ridge. I thought I'd been unobserved but the first slug chipped a rock fragment from in front of my feet while the second ripped a long sliver from the boulder near my head as I got into cover.

My heart was thumping heavily and my hand was definitely unsteady as I checked the Smith-Wesson; I guessed Pacelli was holed up in a triangle of boulders grouped at the lip of the gorge about a hundred feet ahead. I worked my way round to the right of my boulder only to find it ended in air; the drop was sheer here and I could see vicious-looking needles of rock standing up like cathedrals from a projecting ridge about two hundred feet farther down.

I worked back to the left again, fired two slugs toward the triangle, heard them smack satisfyingly into rock; under cover of that I ran toward the outer edge of the mass, hoping Pacelli would still have his head down. He didn't react this time so I guessed he'd quitted the position. I went to ground in a tangled area of rocks and stunted shrubbery where the wind was a good deal colder, coming off the great open space of the gorge.

I got to my hands and knees, working forward a foot at a time, the Smith-Wesson up ready. There was nothing in the centre of the triangle except a mass of wavering shadow, the very worst kind of terrain. The pitted surface of the ridge was littered with boulders just big enough to conceal a man. I stayed where I was, working out the thing in my mind.

The sun was stencilling the moving shadows of the trees and shrubs on to the surface of the rocks and it was so dim in the area bounded by the boulders that it took me a little while to satisfy myself the space was empty. Then I saw the blue-grey depths of a large fissure that led away to the right, toward the edge of the gorge.

I guessed maybe Pacelli had taken that route and a few moments later I heard a minute scraping sound and then the clittering of loose scree over the harsh surface of the rock. I was in no hurry now and I took another five minutes to cover the ground to the edge of the chimney. It was a deadly place and only someone as desperate as Pacelli would have tried it.

I went around the top, skirting it, and came back on the far side, searching the gorge below. Pacelli had chosen the place well; there was a big overhang here and I wouldn't be able to spot him until he was well down the mountainside; there was a lot of shadowy, broken ground there, where he could work his way back and eventually link up with his getaway car. A professional always had a back-up.

I could see the layby, a far scratch in the distance and there, by the side of the toy automobile, the solitary black figure of the driver. It was too far away to see properly but I guessed he might be watching the top of the gorge with binoculars.

I went back to the edge of the chimney,

looking down at the precipitous angle and the sharp pinnacles of rock below. I put the Smith-Wesson back in the holster. It seemed to be the day for madness. I grabbed a knob of rock with none too steady fingers and levered myself over into space.

2

The going wasn't as bad as I feared. My biggest problem was in case Pacelli should appear below me blasting before I could get into a less suicidal position. But it didn't happen and I guessed he maybe had his own troubles lower down; if the second diagonal of the chimney was as rugged as this one he would have problems, certainly no hand free to fire at me.

It was one of the worst ten minutes of my life but I got on to a small projecting platform of rock in the end and wriggled cautiously forward, keeping my head low. The chimney led off in two directions now; to the right was a shadowy ridge, a continuation of the chimney just below it. I knew Pacelli wouldn't have gone that way for the simple reason that the knob of rock on which I was perched commanded a view all its length.

Only a man keen on suicide would have crawled down there where he would have been at the mercy of any viewer. As if to reinforce my reasoning I heard another furtive rockfall, coming from a long way down, in the crooked crack below me to the left. I was over into the shadow without hesitation.

The going was much easier here and I was able to get into the side of the ridge, with its great humped nodules of rock, and almost walk down, watching carefully the area below, and clinging on to the outcrops with my two hands. It would have made any real mountaineer laugh but I was in the butchery business today and not the Alpine stuff.

I still couldn't see anything but in a little while I came out on a cleared space of granite outcrop where I could turn round and face downward. The wind was whipping here, feeling cool and tempering the terrific heat that was coming off the rocks. I supposed it was something to do with the thermals and whether the air was blowing from the areas in shadow or directly in the sun.

I paused a moment or two, sweat dripping off me. I got the Smith-Wesson out again and laid it down on the rock within easy reach of my hand. From here I could see the sheer drop down to the projecting pinnacles. They didn't look any less murderous or precipitous. From there the terrain fell away in steep humps, each several hundred feet deep, like gigantic steps, to the mass of scree and rubble that was hidden in the distant blueness of the shadowy base.

Immediately below me was another tumbled area of boulders and deep grooves that had obviously been driven in the solid rock by the rains over hundreds, maybe countless thousands of years. It was dark and shadowy too and gave off an aura of menace. It was as nasty a place as I'd seen and ideal for Pacelli to hole up. It would be suicide to venture down in there without first making sure exactly where my man was.

I pulled my head back in and thought out my next move. Far away to the right I could see the twisting thread of the road and the dusty layby. The black automobile, looking as minute and insignificant as a beetle at the bottom of an elevator shaft was still there; the motionless figure of the driver standing a short distance away but the distance was too great to make out detail.

I heard another scrabbling noise then. I put my head up, reaching for the Smith-Wesson. The slug that should have taken my head off split the rock-face a foot or two above, driving fine splinters into my eyes and scaring the hell out of me. I let off a shot in reply, more as a reflex than anything else. The slug must have gone up in the air but it gave me some feeling of satisfaction.

I couldn't see him for the moment but Pacelli must have been holed up in the jumble of boulders that made a jagged formation against the sky-line. I wriggled back a little, getting my face as far down into the rock as I could. I felt desperately exposed here though the feeling was irrational and ridiculous.

Pacelli was below me, in fact, but I'd been up at the edge of this ridge and my head would have been momentarily silhouetted against the far rocks, giving the hidden hit-man a better target.

I lay there for what seemed an age but in reality could not have been more than ten minutes.

I heard another scraping noise then and the tension seemed to leak out of the air; it was a crazy term to use, even to myself, but other people who've ever been in the same situation will know what I mean. It meant that Pacelli had quitted the shelter of the boulders and was probably trying to find his way down the far rim that led into the gorge below.

It took all the will-power I could summon but I made sure there was no-one in sight and swung myself down into the hollow among the boulders and detritus of ages, keeping in the deep shadow, the crown of rocks climbing up above me now at an impossible angle. I mentally saluted Pacelli's own toughness then because he'd had to come down in here and up the other side, knowing that any moment I might show behind him to put a bullet in his shoulder-blades.

I could hear the scraping once more, like someone's heels cautiously testing out the rock surface. I knew Pacelli was too occupied in finding a way down off the ledge in the cul-de-sac he'd gotten into to bother about me. He might even figure he'd taken me out. I put the Smith-Wesson in the waistband of my trousers and used both hands to lever myself quietly up toward the boulders.

In another five minutes I was in among them, moving around cautiously, trying not to make any noise. When I finally made the rim of the largest I felt bushed. At first, when I looked downward, I couldn't see anything. Then I heard the scraping noise again. Pacelli was below me, beneath an overhang. The angle was so fantastic I couldn't see his body. I got the Smith-Wesson and put it away then. I knew I wasn't going to need it.

'You can't get out, Pacelli,' I said. 'You might as well give up.'

The shot and the angle was an impossible one but he'd tried it. He held on to the rock with one hand and loosed off a shell with the other. The recoil had thrown him off balance and I heard the pistol clatter against granite as his desperately clutching fingers scrabbled ineffectually at the rock face.

His feet went then and he slid to the outer rim of the rock; he went over almost inch by inch until only his head, shoulders and straining hands were left. His eyes were raised to mine; he'd tried to kill me and he'd probably taken the garage attendant out but I felt I'd never forget their expression. But he was still the professional beneath the tortured mask.

The thin lips writhed back over the white, even teeth, below the heavy black mustache.

'Get me out, Faraday,' he said in a dead voice. 'I'll make it worth your while.'

Then he said something, the significance of which only came to me later.

'After all, we're on the same side.'

I eased down the edge of the boulder as far as I dared. I took off my jacket, held it toward him by one sleeve.

'Grab that with your right hand,' I said.

It was about four inches short. I had my left hand jammed in a crack in the boulders and I couldn't get any farther down without losing my own balance. There was a deathly silence now and I was conscious of a kite planing along in the clear air about a thousand feet away.

The safety of the earth; the twisting ribbon of road and Pacelli's black getaway car might have been a million miles off for all the good they were going to do him.

His strength seemed to be failing. He cast a desperate look up to me and made a supreme effort. The whole of his body was dangling in space now, supported by his two hands. He raised himself slightly, his outstretched right hand still a good two inches below the dangling material of the sleeve. He gave a startled little cry and then he was gone, turning over and over, his body rapidly diminishing in the blueness of space.

He must have been dead as soon as he struck the first pinnacle but he kept tumbling over and over at a dizzy speed, striking first one, then another, the sun shining on blandly; the kite still circling; the air fresh and pure with the smell of the mountains. I watched him until the mangled mass was out of sight. The clittering progress of the scree seemed to go on for a long time after.

All my limbs were trembling now, the sleeve of my jacket whipping in the breeze. The ant down on the faint scratch of the road had left his position. He got back into the black automobile and it presently crawled out of sight. I lay there for what seemed like a long time. I felt cold and I had a job to co-ordinate my movements.

I found my jacket still clutched tightly in the reflexive grip of my right hand. It was fixed so tight I had a job to unclench it. It took me a hell of a lot longer to put the jacket on and button it. Then I started to crawl back out of that shadowy pit.

I fell back three times, though it was an easy climb with a drop beneath, over a gentle slope, of no more than fifteen feet. When I finally made it to the top of the ridge I was drenched with sweat and as blown as an ancient cab-horse. The sun beat heavily and dully on my head as I walked like a drunk man slowly and painfully back up toward where I figured Praegar's must be.

I heard the noises long before I got there and there was the wail of a police siren now. The wind was agitating the branches of the screening trees and I had to go along quite a way before I found the place I'd come through. The parking lot was black with people and the edge of the railing lined with the pale ovals of faces. The crowd gave a ragged cheer as I came in sight though what the hell for I didn't know; I might well have been Pacelli for all they knew.

I went across and looked at the gap I'd jumped earlier and had to sit down. Presently a voice penetrated. I made it out to belong to Kettle. He was apparently saying to stay put. He needn't have bothered. I had no intention of going anywhere until they built a bridge or something equally substantial.

I sat there with the sun hot on my head, the noise of the crowd a blurred muddle in my ears until the fire brigade showed and god-like men in scarlet helmets started winching out an escape ladder. It was an anti-climax after what had happened but it was the only way they were going to get me off there.

CHAPTER NINETEEN

1

It was early evening when I got to Pepper Coburn's house. She lived up in one of the canyons on the outskirts of Beverly Hills and my limbs were aching so much I felt like an old man of eighty. It had been a long session out at Praegar's. Kettle had been more understanding than I figured. And the police had been pretty helpful under the circumstances; especially after Kettle's explanations.

I'd phoned in to Stella and gone back to Park West to change my clothes and have a shower. I'd taped up my cuts and scratches and the bruises would have to look after themselves. I'd had some time to think after the Pacelli shoot-out and a lot of loose ends kept coming back to me. Things that I should have figured before if my brain hadn't been so addled with the sapping.

They were mostly to do with the death of the mechanic; and something that Pacelli had said just before he went off the ledge kept floating in and out of what was left of my mind. I hoped Pepper Coburn would have some of the answers. She would know about Stoltz' death by now; it had been on several radio newscasts and the early evening editions had a brief front page story.

The sun had almost set behind the hills and there were long shadows on the ground as I drew up in front of the large Spanish-style bungalow with the tasteful statuary in the grounds. It had been raining here earlier but it was drying nicely now and the air had that cool freshness that the evening sometimes brings in Southern California.

Birds were singing mournfully beyond the flowering hedges and I had all the weight of the world on my shoulders as I got out the Buick and slammed the driving door. The hollow thud sounded like earth falling on a coffin lid. It was one of my recurring similes but then my cases often bring such things to mind. My shirt was sticking to my back as I went up the crazy paved pathway between the statuary and the shaved lawns with the perfume of tropical flowers in my nostrils, the Smith-Wesson a heavy weight in its harness.

My ring was answered by a smartly-dressed Filipino maid. Miss Coburn was home but she was resting. I said I understood her feelings but I'd come about Stoltz. The girl had a faint puffiness of the eyes like she'd been crying but she opened her mouth wide at that. It was an ironic situation; Stoltz and the girl planning to take Kettle out but the scheme rebounding on them both. I didn't know why I was here really. But I like tidy ends and as I said there were things gnawing at me.

I hadn't told the police about the boy at the garage, of course. That would have been asking for trouble. And I had to be free to operate. I'd get to it later. When I'd got everything straight in my mind. If that time ever came.

The girl had gone now, leaving me in a tasteful black and white tiled hall where some excellent eighteenth-century English oil paintings of Norfolk landscapes floated out against the pale cream walls. I'm no art expert but they looked to be of the school of Crome and Cotman. If they'd been Constables I guess the girl wouldn't have left me alone in the place.

She re-appeared in a few minutes. Her eyes were troubled and curious as they searched my face.

'Miss Coburn will see you in a short while, Mr Faraday. Will you follow me, please'.

She led me along a narrow corridor to a pleasant, panelled room with a lot of comfortable furniture, whose large French windows looked out on to the green wilderness of the garden.

I had only been there a couple of minutes before Pepper Coburn came in. Contrary to what I expected she was restrained and obviously shaken but there was none of the grief and anger that I had expected. She shook hands briskly, throwing the dark hair back from her forehead and moved over toward a drinks cabinet.

'I'm surprised to see you here, Mr Faraday, after the news bulletins. You should have been in for a hospital check following your experiences today.'

'Anyone sensible would have,' I said.

She smiled briefly, opening the lid of the cabinet.

'You'd like something strong to soothe your nerves?'

'Fine,' I said.

She handed me Scotch and water in a long glass with ice and busied herself at the cabinet mixing her own drink.

'I don't usually indulge this time of the afternoon but the circumstances are out of the ordinary. The police have already been here. My fiance is flying in from Miami tonight.'

My surprise must have shown on my face because the Coburn number shot me a wry look and went to sit on the end of a leather divan, waving me into an easy chair opposite.

'You're puzzled, Mr Faraday. But you mustn't believe all the studio publicity you read. Herman Stoltz was a good friend and I'm naturally shocked and cut up about his death. But we were business associates, nothing more.'

The ratchets of my mind went on turning uselessly, without engaging in anything. The interview was developing so differently from what I expected that I was momentary thrown.

'I can't imagine why anyone would want to kill him. Or Mr Kettle for that matter. I understand you were engaged by Mr Kettle following some sort of threats he'd received. I know nothing of such matters and I don't see how I can help you. So far as I understand it from the police the case is closed.'

I shook my head.

'On the contrary, Miss Coburn, it's just beginning.'

2

The tall brunette put her two hands together round the stem of her crystal goblet and creased up her eyes as she stared at me. She was all in white; white silk shirt, white linen slacks and white high heel shoes. She wore an unusual string of scarlet beads round her neck and they set off the effect in a striking manner.

'Naturally, I'll help all I can, Mr Faraday, but I can't imagine what you're getting at. Herman and I often held business meetings up at Praegar's. In fact it was a favourite place of ours because we could talk and study plans. And it was only a short distance away from the Sunset Homes development in which I have a considerable financial interest.'

I stared at her for a long moment. This was getting more interesting by the minute.

'Tell me about Mr Kettle,' I said. 'Why would anyone want to kill him?'

The tall brunette frowned again. It was an absolute close-up from one of her earlier movies. It was a favourite of mine. And a murder mystery too. She shook her head.

'I can't imagine. He and Mr Stoltz were the best of friends. So far as I know they'd never had a cross word, unlike most business partners. Except that Herman had occasionally to warn him about his gambling.'

I felt a faint stirring in the hairs on the nape of my neck. It's something that happens when hunches start crystallising.

'And you would have known if there was bad blood between them,' I said quickly. 'As you were in such close contact with Mr Stoltz.'

She nodded.

'Harry Kettle's an inveterate gambler, Mr Faraday. Once or twice Mr Stoltz confided to me that he was a little worried about his partner's business stability. He had to talk to him about it on occasion.'

Her face cleared.

'I see. You think that some gambling interests to whom Harry owed money may have tried to take him out?'

The ratchets in my mind went on whirring.

'It's possible,' I said.

I decided to level with Pepper Coburn. She was so transparently honest in what she was saying and I believed her absolutely. Even the best actress in the world couldn't have overlaid her grief in this way if she and Stoltz had been like Kettle had told me. Which reversed the entire situation.

'Kettle was worried,' I said. 'In fact I kept tabs on both partners for a while. I was at the restaurant a couple of days back when you and Herman Stoltz were having lunch there. I thought you were in love with one another.'

The tall brunette stared at me incredulously, a faint flush rising to the roots of her hair. Then she threw back her head and let out a throaty gurgle.

'You were a million miles wide of the truth, Mr Faraday. As I recall it, apart from business matters, we were mostly talking about my fiance. We're getting married next month, you know. And to the best of my knowledge poor Herman was still paying alimony to his estranged wife back in the East. So he wouldn't have been really anxious to get married again.'

All the pieces that had fallen apart in my mind were beginning to come together again now, only in different positions; like a puzzle that someone had cut up with a fretsaw and re-jigged to make an entirely opposite pattern. I was glad the girl had started the conversation and not me.

Looked at from the opposite angle everything started to fit; even what Pacelli had said made sense. I would have been on his side as I was working for Kettle. I'd sort the details out later. I decided I might as well take a dive off the deep-end while I was at it. Pepper Coburn was so outward-giving and honest that she wouldn't take offence at a little more probing on my part.

'I understood you and Herman Stoltz and Harry Kettle and Elizabeth Goddard made up foursomes occasionally.'

The Coburn number swilled the drink moodily around in the bottom of her goblet, her violet-coloured eyes fixed on my face.

'That's true to a certain extent, Mr Faraday. They were mostly business gatherings in fact. That was what concerned us all. We made up an occasional foursome for dinner, if that's what you mean.'

She smiled faintly.

'Liz Goddard and I met more frequently than the others, I guess. We both belong to the same rifle club. And she was a movie actress too, was she not?'

Another ratchet whirred and then clicked sweetly into position.

'Come again?' I said.

Pepper Coburn's smile widened.

'I can see you're old-fashioned, Mr Faraday. You don't believe in rifle-shooting females.'

I gave her one of my best battered grins.

'I wouldn't exactly say that, Miss Coburn. I find women dangerous enough already, without putting weapons in their hands.'

Pepper Coburn went on smiling. I could have watched it all evening. The smoothness of the Scotch was beginning to ease the raw edges of my aches and pains away.

'There'd be no danger with Liz Goddard, Mr Faraday. She's deadly accurate; way out of my class. In fact it wouldn't be an exaggeration to say she's one of the best shots in the L.A. basin.'

I smiled again.

'That's all I wanted to know, Miss Coburn.'

I'd learned more in casual conversation with her in ten minutes than in several days of gum-shoeing around in the rain and getting my brains knocked out. In more senses than one. In fact I needed my head examined.

The Coburn number still sat on the arm of the divan looking at me with those extraordinary eyes. I felt like I was playing a minor part in one of her own movies.

'Is there anything else I can tell you, Mr Faraday? I don't think I've been of very much help.'

I got up and held out my unoccupied hand.

'On the contrary, Miss Coburn, you've been the greatest help in the world.'

CHAPTER TWENTY

1

It was after eight when I reached the Innes Court Apartments. It was a fine clear night like the last time I was here. It seemed a million years ago now. When one's perspective changes it alters the way solid things look; even the air, the senses of taste and smell. That was probably stale James Joyce but it was the way I felt tonight. And if I hadn't called in at Pepper Coburn's maybe I would never have gotten the right slant.

The three ornamental fountains in the tiled concourse still had the naked marble nymphs frolicking in the falling columns of water. I drove the Buick into the darkest corner of the parking lot and killed the motor. I remembered the armed commissionaire in his glass box at the main entrance and decided to make my own way up to Kettle's place. I'd rather enter unannounced this time.

I was tired of being the patsy and I'd rather face Stella after I got a few more answers. I'd missed out by a ratio of about 99.9 per cent so far.

I worked my way round the fringe of the parking lot, looking for another way up to the main building. There was a small stair at the side, under the deep shadow of the trees. The main entrance to the apartments was way over to my left now, the only illumination here coming from the parking lot lights set atop their steel poles. Providing there were no TV monitors or electronic alarms where I was going I had a good chance of making it to the penthouse. But if the service elevator wasn't working tonight I had a long walk in front of me.

For once I was in luck. I gum-shoed down a cement path in back of a tall hedge. The path led around the building and in a couple of minutes I got to a heavy metal door marked: SERVICE ENTRANCE. One half the door was latched back, maybe because it was a warm night; or more likely because a delivery truck was expected some time in the evening.

Lights burned along the corridor inside and I could see there was no-one around. There was an elevator up the far end and the silhouette of a metal staircase balustrade to the right, opposite the elevator cage. I glanced down toward the parking lot. Apart from the traffic noise and the lights of passing automobiles there was no-one around; on foot, that is.

I eased into the passage, aware now of the noise of a radio or TV set coming from a half-open door farther down. I could see without the painted legend that it led to the janitor's quarters. This might be tricky. I was almost up to the door now when I heard someone clear his throat. It's strange how you can pick out a noise emanating somewhere around you from a mechanically reproduced sound from radio or TV.

I risked a peek. The white-haired man in the easy chair had his back to me, watching TV. I got quickly and quietly past and went silently up the lower treads of the staircase. I was resigned to the long walk. Any use of the service elevator would be bound to bring the old man out; the whine of the motor would be unmistakable, even over the racket his programme was making.

I walked up three flights, listening to the steady pumping of my heart, conscious of the reassuring pressure of the Smith-Wesson against my shoulder muscles. The faint sound of the TV died away; then there was nothing in the bleak concrete stairwell but the almost inaudible progress of my feet on the rubber composition treads.

I stopped on the third-floor landing, tempted to get out and use the tenants' elevator; then I decided against. I wanted to try something else tonight with the intention of achieving surprise. I didn't hang around. Instead, I kept on walking, my mind still turning over, but making more sense now; unconscious of the monotony of the physical slog to the top.

It must have taken me almost half an hour

and my leg muscles were aching when I got level with the penthouse suites; now there was nothing but the distant hum of air-conditioning. I took a glance through the small glass port in the staircase door; there was the concourse with Penthouse No. 4 almost alongside. I got back on the landing of the service stairs, staring at the small door which had FIRE EXIT on it in large red letters.

It would have to be unlocked because of regulations. I opened it, blinking at the smog and the neon-dazzle of L.A. spread out below; the noise of traffic hit one like a wave up here, probably funnelled by the bare front of the building; accentuated by the wind which was gusting on the exposed metal platform. I got out, closing the door to the staircase firmly behind me.

I guessed the penthouse walls and the greenery would muffle the noise up on the terrace; they'd evidently been designed with that object in view. The metal stair leading off the platform went on up top and I eased up tread by tread, making sure there were no squeaky ones. After a few yards I came out on a catwalk which ran along beneath the penthouse balconies.

I could see lights gleaming among the greenery now. Like I figured there were smaller metal ladders screwed to the façade of the building, giving access to the railed-in balcony I was on. I went up the nearest; I

194

couldn't see much at the top because of the greenery but it had to be Kettle's terrace because of the physical lay-out and I recognised the design of one of the lanterns gleaming through the tangle of vines.

I knew the fittings were different from the neighbours because I'd noticed on my last visit. There was another short ladder stapled to the wall the far side and I got over the brickwork and went down it quickly, hand over hand. I was on a narrow cement path on the opposite side of the carp-pool, shielded by a screen of shrubbery. I had the Smith-Wesson out now and I walked along carefully, listening to the distant murmur of voices above the night noises of the city.

I got as far forward as I dared, conscious that Kettle was sitting at one of the cane tables just the other side the pool. He had somebody with him but I couldn't make who because he was sitting just beyond a fringe of foliage.

I eased into a position where I could see and hear Kettle more clearly. He was smoking a cigar, puffing out blue clouds which went up waveringly into the evening air and he looked pleased with himself.

He was counting a bundle of greenbacks on the table in front of him, moving his lips now without any sound coming out. That annoyed me for a start because I hate people who do that.

The other person spoke then. It was a man's

voice and vaguely familiar, though I couldn't place it for a moment.

'And Faraday?'

'He did a good job,' Kettle said. 'He's settled Pacelli. Things came out very neatly.'

I grinned and shifted a little closer. That was the clincher. It was coming out fine. I threw off the safety of the Smith-Wesson. Kettle was flicking the bundle of bills across the table. The second man leaned forward then, to pick them up. I found myself looking at the fat, greasy face of Perrot.

2

He sat with one pudgy finger over the bills as I stepped out the shrubbery and looked at him from the other side of the pool. His right hand, the one in the shadow, darted down to his side.

'I wouldn't try it,' I said.

Perrot licked his lips and glanced at Kettle as though it was his turn to take over. Kettle sat with both hands steady on the table-top. He looked subtly different from the harassed, fearful man I'd known. I remembered then he was an actor. They were all actors, come to that. His eyes flickered briefly to me and then back to the fat man again.

'Wouldn't you have found it easier to come in the normal way, Mr Faraday?'

'Maybe,' I said. 'But then I wouldn't have

got the right side of the story.'

'It took you some time, even for a stupid private dick,' the fat man spat out.

His eyes glittered with rage and his ham-like fists were clenched into balls.

'It always does,' I said. 'But I usually get there in the end.'

Kettle had a weary expression on his face.

'I wish I knew what you were talking about, Mr Faraday,' he said. 'Wouldn't you be more comfortable over here with us.'

'Maybe,' I said. 'I'll come round. Just remember the bushes are thin here. I can shoot through them well enough in case you try anything fancy.'

Kettle shrugged.

'Just why should I do anything like that, Mr Faraday? I have achieved my object.'

I didn't answer that. I was circling quickly now, steadying up behind Perrot's broad back. Kettle sat on at the table. He wore a scarlet open-neck shirt and white linen slacks and I didn't figure he would be armed. It was Perrot I had to watch and I had two fairly thick tree trunks to negotiate before I got on their side of the pool.

I bent quickly, found a sizeable rock that was edging the path. I hefted it into the pool. It made a heavy splash, drenching and startling the two men, both of whom ducked under the table. I was round their side now, jammed the Smith-Wesson in Perrot's back.

197

'That was a stupid thing to do,' Kettle said.

'But much safer for me,' I told him.

I tapped the fat man's ear with my gun-barrel.

'Let's have the piece and be quick about it.'

Perrot took the big automatic out his pocket with a grunt. He held it by his little finger through the trigger-guard. His finger was as big as a carrot and he had a job to get it through.

'If it goes off you go off,' I told him.

His shoulders made a convulsive shudder.

'It won't go off,' he promised.

I leaned over and took it from him quickly, moving over to a chair midway between the two. I put my foot up on the chair and levelled the Smith-Wesson, resting my hand on my knee. Kettle paused in mopping water from his soaked shirt. He didn't look at me direct.

'I wish you'd tell us what all this is about, Mr Faraday. I was just telling Mr Perrot here you were due for a bonus for your successful cracking of the case.'

'I'll bet,' I said.

I looked at him closely. His eyes were steady at first but then they wavered.

'You were pretty good,' I said. 'You told me a true story. But you told it the wrong way round. And I fell for it.'

Kettle's expression didn't change. Perrot licked his lips and moved his big carrot fingers on the table top.

'I had forgotten you were an actor,' I said. 'You gave the performance of your life. Elizabeth Goddard was even better. I didn't know she was in movies until tonight. And she was a crack shot too.'

'Get to the point,' Kettle said.

There was a sudden rasping quality to his voice which hadn't been there before.

'I'm getting to it,' I told him. 'You set me up. You gave me a great story. And I swallowed it. Reluctantly at first, but I swallowed it just the same.'

Kettle moved very slightly in his chair and I swivelled the Smith-Wesson barrel. He froze, his eyes looking hurt and incredulous. He did it beautifully but it wasn't going over.

'Your partner knew nothing about any of this,' I said. 'You got on fine. The business was flourishing. And he knew little of your speculative schemes. Plus horses and the lady. Expensive tastes, has she?'

Perrot nodded faintly. He was breathing heavily through his nose.

'Everything you told me about the murder attempts was lies,' I said. 'But you needed me for a reliable witness. And it was almost a hundred carat gold scheme. The acid on the brakes was real. It had to be because the garage was the first place you intended me to go. I was supposed to talk to Perrot but I made the mistake of speaking to the wrong man first. The sandy-haired kid you or Perrot killed.'

199

Kettle was moved to protest. His eyes were smouldering.

'What is all this?'

'As if you didn't know,' I said. 'I was slow, of course. You were frightened for your life. Stoltz' hitman was going to blast you. Instead of which Pacelli was working for you. And making himself highly visible to me. You intended to take out Stoltz all along. You murdered him in a public restaurant with hundreds of people looking on with me as the star witness for the defence.'

I stared at the two men thoughtfully. They didn't move a muscle; they might have been wax dummies at the table in the mellow light of the overhead lanterns.

'So you didn't mind when I took Pacelli out,' I said. 'One of you would have to have taken him out anyway, because he knew too much. Maybe Mr Greenstreet here. That was you waiting with the sedan at the bottom of the gorge, wasn't it? I wondered why Pacelli said we were both on the same side; it only came to me later.'

'A lot of things seem to have come to you later,' Kettle said. 'I only wish I knew what you were talking about. And just exactly how you're going to prove all this fantasy . . .'

'I'll make it stick,' I said. 'You got me to follow Pacelli—faked up that correspondence at Chiltern Stationery Supplies. One of your subsidiaries, right?'

I tapped the pocket which contained Perrot's pistol.

'Ballistics will help,' I told Kettle. 'You had Liz Goddard up at Stoltz' place that night, dressed in men's clothes. She fired to miss me, to add to the general plausibility of your story. Well, I bought that too; it built up the atmosphere and suggested perhaps another group was trying to take your partner out. The other incidents you mentioned relied on your testimony or that of Miss Goddard, with no other witnesses. It was nicely done. I couldn't prove or disprove anything—and I couldn't speak to Stoltz.'

I tapped my pocket again.

'Tests on Perrot's pistol might prove something. I figure you shot the sandy-haired boy when he came to warn me.'

I swivelled the barrel of the .38 gently, soothing down the faint impatience the two men at the table were beginning to show. I was getting hoarse with all this talking.

'That made no sense at all. Because Mr Greenstreet here didn't know me or my address. Nor the boy. He could only have got it from you. That lets you in, Kettle. My guess is you and Perrot were talking over the situation, perhaps in your office at the garage and the boy overheard. He tried to warn me and one of you took him out. Which one is irrelevant for the moment. It certainly had nothing to do with the damage to the Rolls.'

I glanced about the gleaming elegance of the terrace.

'We only want Miss Goddard to make the party complete. Where is she, by the way?'

'Here, Mr Faraday,' said a soft voice from the shadow of the pool-side trees.

The gun blasted with a noise like a traffic back-fire as I dived across the terrace into the shelter of the undergrowth.

CHAPTER TWENTY-ONE

1

Jagged fire ran down my right arm from the shoulder, and the Smith-Wesson fell from my stiffening fingers and skittered across the tiling. Perrot's massive figure rose with astonishing swiftness and planted a huge foot on it. I hit the edge of an ornamental flower bed with an impact that drove the breath from my body. I was lying half-in, half-out the heavy shadow.

I reached for Perrot's pistol, took it out and laid it down in the edge of the flower bed. I had one of the large brown rocks from the border now. I held it in the palm of my hand; it might do at a pinch, if I did it quickly enough. The girl had eased out from the shadow. She was coming round the edge of the pool while

Perrot covered me with the Smith-Wesson.

'The pistol, Faraday,' he gritted. 'Or you get it now.'

I was still in deep shadow. I made a show of reluctance and hefted the rock with my left hand. It made a heavy splash in the centre of the pool. The water was dark in the middle and there was nothing to be seen.

I dragged myself a foot or two away from where the big automatic was hidden, resting my back against the trunk of a palm, like I was bushed. I saw blood trickling down my right wrist. The girl was standing in front of me. She looked at me with reluctance in her eyes.

'You were a fool, Mr Faraday. You could have taken your fee and stepped out. The case is closed.'

I shook my head.

'That wouldn't be right, Miss Goddard. You know as well as I do that in all good B-pictures the baddies always get their come-uppance in Reel 8.'

The girl gave me a bitter smile and joined Kettle, who'd gotten up from the table. Perrot was standing close now. He looked as big as a forty-ton truck. He stepped nearer and kicked me three times in the ribs. Kettle took the pistol from the girl, his cigar smoke wavering in the night air.

'That will do,' he said sharply. 'Save it for later. There may be people on the other balconies.'

Perrot stepped away. I must have momentarily blacked out because I felt something trickling down my face. The girl was kneeling by my side with a crystal water jug. There was real regret in her eyes.

'You were a fool, Mr Faraday.'

'You already said that,' I told her.

'All right, Faraday,' Kettle said. 'You proved your point. We played it like you said. But where does that get you, except dead.'

He shrugged.

'So you've been talking to Pepper Coburn. Well, that figures. It was the only real loose end but we had to risk it. And once you've disappeared she won't be able to prove anything even if she is suspicious. She has other things to think about. She's getting married soon.'

'So she told me,' I said. 'But what makes you think I'm going to disappear. I intend to remain highly visible.'

Perrot gave a harsh, vibrating laugh that seemed to start echoes from the terrace tiling and send little ripples across the surface of the pool.

'I thought you were the comedian,' he told Kettle.

I sagged back against the palm trunk, letting Liz Goddard fuss with my arm. She'd eased off my jacket, was binding a handkerchief round the wound. From the way it was hurting I knew it was clean; it had gone through flesh without touching bone. I wanted to stay by the palm as long as possible; that was my only chance.

'I'll go get the car,' Perrot said.

Kettle shook his head, stopped the other with a violent movement of his hand.

'We got to think the situation out. We can't get him through the lobby like this.'

Liz Goddard passed the wet cloth across my face thoughtfully. The touch seemed to erase the pain. She licked her lips.

'And there's a janitor at the service entrance,' she reminded Kettle.

He went back to sit at the table. The girl started putting my jacket on. Perrot stood near me, holding the Smith-Wesson down at his side. His eyes glittered but that was the only sign of life about his huge bulk.

'Maybe he could have an accident,' he said. 'In the pool here?'

Kettle's eyes were patient beneath the dyed red hair as he lifted his head.

'Leave the thinking to me,' he said softly.

The girl got up quickly. I noticed the unusual ring on her finger again. It reminded me of the time in the office when I'd thought she was fine and clean-boned and a great little executive. She was all of that still. That and other things.

'Perrot has a point,' she told Kettle. 'But not this pool. From the fire-escape atop the building into the fountain would obliterate most of the damage.'

Kettle gave a heavy sigh.

'For a dame with education you come out with some stupid ideas, sometimes,' he said. 'He has a bullet-hole in his arm, right? So he tried to commit suicide before diving off the building. That brings us to the pistol.'

The girl bit her lip.

'We could leave it on the terrace.'

Even Perrot stared at her incredulously.

'And have it match up with the slug you put in Barnes,' he said. 'The pressure's getting to you, kid. You'd both best leave the thinking to me.'

I figured Barnes was the sandy-haired boy who'd tried to warn me. Had warned me, come to that. If I could get the girl's pistol I had the complete picture. It lay on the table. It was on the side farthest away from Kettle. He wouldn't be able to get to it in a hurry. And I knew he wasn't armed. That left Perrot with the Smith-Wesson. The safety was off and I knew he hadn't put it back on.

I looked at Elizabeth Goddard thoughtfully, thinking of the boy's mangled chest. How he'd managed to hold together to get to my place I'd never know. All the police would need would be the lab tests on the girl's pistol. Plus my testimony. That meant both of us had to be around when things came to court. And that would depend on my physical shape and the events of the next half-hour. In the meantime I lay still and gave my well-known impression of a very beat-up P.I.

'Could we use one of those big wheeled laundry baskets?' Perrot said. 'I saw one in the corridor on a lower floor coming up.'

Kettle raised his eyes to the night sky of L.A.

'I'm surrounded by clowns,' he said.

'You should give a master-class.' I told him.

Kettle got up suddenly. For such a small man he looked almost tall. But maybe that was because I was lying on the terrace. Perrot and the girl were looking at him now. There would never be a better opportunity.

I put out my left hand in the shadow, found the pistol. The gesture was natural, as though I were trying to support myself. I managed to transfer it to my left-hand jacket pocket. The others were too intent on Kettle to notice my minute movements in the darkness.

'Shouldn't be too difficult,' Kettle said. 'We take him down the fire escape. Then we waste him in the mountains.'

2

Perrot's five chins wobbled slightly so that I was again reminded of some historical character with lace at his throat. His silvering hair glistened under the lamplight as he lifted the Smith-Wesson. I suddenly felt very tired and the ache in my ribs where the fat man had kicked me was beginning to bother me. I hoped he hadn't broken anything.

With the hole in my arm it could make things tricky. I'd have to use the pistol with my left in any case. As I'm right-handed that would be difficult enough. I'd meet that when I got to it. Like always.

The rings on Perrot's fingers glistened like knuckle-dusters as he gestured with the Smith-Wesson.

'Time to go, Faraday.'

I sagged forward like I was all in. The huge man put one hand under my left armpit and hauled me to my feet like I was a feather-weight. I decided not to under-estimate him. I stumbled and almost fell and he had to hold me up for a moment.

'What about the heap?' he asked Kettle.

The red-haired man rubbed his fingers across his chin.

'Liz will fetch it once we get down. She'll drive and we'll sit in back.'

He nodded at the girl.

'I'll go get my jacket. Meanwhile you move him the other side the pool. And take care. He's a tricky customer.'

The sneer on Perrot's face would have taken the talents of a master painter to register.

'He won't be doing any fancy stuff,' he told Kettle.

The girl stood back from me, picking up the

pistol from the table.

'I'm pretty good with this, Mr Faraday. Don't make me do it here.'

'I won't,' I said.

Perrot's muddy eyes above the dark mustache looked at me with a dead expression. The unusual signet ring with the emerald on Elizabeth Goddard's finger glittered as coldly as the smile on her face as she gently held it against the trigger. She still wore the high-gloss bouffant hair-style but now it looked as artificial as everything else about her and I wondered why I had ever found her attractive.

She motioned me forward. Perrot's grip on my left arm tightened and he hustled me through the undergrowth on to the cement path that circled the carp-pool. My size nines gritted on the surface and I was careful not to lean against him, making sure that the heavy bulk of the pistol in my jacket pocket wouldn't bump against him.

But Perrot was being careful too. He was wary and kept me at arm's length, like he was worried I might try some judo routine. Not that I wouldn't have if I'd fancied my chances. But Perrot must have weighed somewhere around twenty stone. He merely had to fall on me to crush me into the concrete. And the girl had the pistol in rear. We were beyond the two mature trees now and I could see Kettle coming back across the terrace the other side the pool, buttoning his white linen jacket.

I stumbled again and immediately felt the barrel of the girl's cannon jabbing into my spine.

'Don't make me do it,' she repeated.

'You mean to say you aren't going to offer me any tea this evening,' I said.

Kettle had joined us now, his feet grating on the cement path.

'You're right, Harry,' the Goddard number said. 'I begin to find his humour trying.'

'You won't have to suffer it much longer,' he said.

'That's right,' I told him. 'At least two murders should earn you forty years apiece. By the way, I forgot to ask. Do I get to keep the retainer?'

Perrot sighed. He let go my arm. His hambone fist, balled tightly, came over and tapped me alongside the head. I almost blacked out. I decided to waste him straight away if I got the chance. The more I thought about it the more difficult it seemed. Especially as the girl was such a good shot.

We were the far side the shrubbery now, up against the brick wall near the ladder where I'd come in. The scenery had been buckling to and fro but it was coming into focus again.

'It was you hit me on the head,' I said. 'Not Pacelli.'

Perrot sniggered. It sounded obscene there in the darkness of the garden.

'Just keeping in practice, Faraday,' he said.

He pushed me up the ladder, still holding on to the bottom of my jacket. He had enormous strength and I had no intention of tangling with him on the fire escapes. That was the easy way to instant suicide. I had to take him if I was to come out myself. And to do that I had to make sure Liz Goddard was blind on her gun hand side at the critical moment.

I got my leg over the top of the brick parapet, found the rung of the corresponding ladder. Perrot slightly relaxed his hold. His head had now appeared above the top, the Smith-Wesson barrel looking as big as the entrance to a freeway tunnel. I stepped down into the windy L.A. night, the dusky glitter of the city spread out below me.

3

I went over to the edge of the balcony, looking down at the bronze figures on the fountain and the parking-lot, squashed and foreshortened at this height.

'Don't go far, Faraday.'

The big man grunted, an edge of anxiety in his voice as he straddled the wall. The .38 barrel wavered slightly. He was only two yards away and I'd missed a chance. But I was beat-up, my arm paining me now. My head ached too. I was hardly in condition to take on the three of them.

I kept facing toward the balcony edge, keeping my left hand away, conscious of the weight of Perrot's pistol in my pocket. It was comparatively dark up here. The three were hardly likely to spot the bulge or the sag in my jacket. They had other things to think about.

Perrot was slowly clambering down the ladder and making heavy weather of it.

'Shall I take the gun for you?' I said.

The fat man shook his head angrily. The girl, at the top of the wall with her pistol, gave me a tight smile.

'You have style, Mr Faraday,' she said grudgingly.

'So do you,' I said. 'Grace under pressure Hemingway called it.'

'You surprise me,' Kettle said.

His head had appeared alongside the girl's. He took the pistol from her as she got on to the ladder. Perrot was down, wheezing as he steadied up the Smith-Wesson.

'I'm full of surprises,' I said.

We waited there while the other two joined us. I was conscious of the coolness and the clearness of the wind on my face after the heat of the day. Perrot motioned me forward. I went along the balcony and started going down the steep metal ladder that led to the floor below. Liz Goddard took the pistol from Kettle again.

I was a little ahead now and it was in shadow here. I sagged toward the metal handrail like I was all beat-up. Perrot came on down, still wheezing. For a brief moment his bulk blocked out the girl and Kettle who were necessarily in single file behind him. He held the revolver away from him as he negotiated the ladder, holding on to the rail with his left hand.

For an instant it was pointed away from me too. In that split-second I had turned to face him, my left hand deep in my pocket. The explosion seemed to take my side off as I fired the automatic through the cloth, the heavy muzzle flash catching my clothing afire. Perrot never knew what hit him. The heavy slug punched clean through him.

The Smith-Wesson clittered on the metal balcony at my feet. I put my shoe on it, crouching, as the big man went sailing over the handrail, still clutching his gut. His muffled scream came long and low and spray rained upward in the floodlighting as he bounced among the bronze figures in the forecourt fountain.

The girl's pistol flamed but she was off balance and wide. I had no time for fancy aiming; my second slug caught her in the left shoulder and swung her round. She screamed then and lifted the pistol toward me. I had the automatic out now, aimed squarely at her body.

'Be sensible,' I said. 'I couldn't miss at this range.'

Kettle's voice was high with rage and fear.

'Drop it, Liz,' he said in trembling tones.

The girl's voice was full of pain and hatred.

'I can take him, Harry.'

'What's the point if he kills you,' Kettle said. 'There's nothing left for us then. Drop it.'

His voice had authority now, like he was speaking to a child. The gun barrel sagged downward. Then Liz Goddard did like he said. The pistol struck the balcony and went over. I'd have the police search for it later. I felt my legs trembling and leaned against the rail.

Below I could see a dark star of blood spreading across the green water of the fountain in the glare of the floods. The girl sat down on one of the metal treads of the staircase. She was crying. Trickles of blood came down her sleeve and dripped from the ends of her fingers. Kettle sat beside her, his arm round her shoulder. He fumbled for a handkerchief, tried to staunch the blood.

There were voices reaching us. Shouts of query and alarm, the sound of running feet. I got a cigarette out my package somehow, using only one hand, keeping the automatic ready for use.

'You killed Perrot,' Kettle said.

'He won't mind,' I told him. 'It was the best thing that ever happened to him.'

Kettle raised his head.

'Can we do a deal, Faraday?'

'No deals,' I said. 'We're going downtown.'

I lit my cigarette shakily, exhaled the smoke. I flipped the used match-stalk down in the direction Perrot had taken. People were clustered as thick as flies round the fountain now. I couldn't see them; only Stella's blonde hair shining in the lamplight. I got down and retrieved the Smith-Wesson. I put it back in my shoulder-holster. I felt properly dressed then.

Liz Goddard went on crying quietly to herself. I guess she was in shock. I didn't waste any thoughts on her. Presently there came the wail of a police siren from the parking-lot below. It seemed a hell of a way down. Kettle was still trying to comfort the blonde girl.

'I love you, Liz. I'll beat the rap somehow. Anything's better than being dead.'

I stared at him, conscious of the night wind on my face; seeing the boy dying in the driving seat; the remains of Herman Stoltz lying under the restaurant table; Pacelli going over the cliff; the surprise on Perrot's face as I blasted him.

'You only die once,' I said.

We hope you have enjoyed this Large Print book. Other Chivers Press or Thorndike Press Large Print books are available at your library or directly from the publishers.

For more information about current and forthcoming titles, please call or write, without obligation, to:

Chivers Large Print
published by BBC Audiobooks Ltd
St James House, The Square
Lower Bristol Road
Bath BA2 3BH
UK
email: bbcaudiobooks@bbc.co.uk
www.bbcaudiobooks.co.uk

OR

Thorndike Press
295 Kennedy Memorial Drive
Waterville
Maine 04901
USA
www.gale.com/thorndike
www.gale.com/wheeler

All our Large Print titles are designed for easy reading, and all our books are made to last.